ONE WOMAN

CRIME WAVE

ONE WOMAN CRIME WAVE

BEE ROWLATT

RENARD PRESS

RENARD PRESS LTD

124 City Road
London EC1V 2NX
United Kingdom
info@renardpress.com
020 8050 2928

www.renardpress.com

One Woman Crime Wave first published by Renard Press Ltd in 2024

Text © Bee Rowlatt, 2024
Quotation on p. 9 © Priestley, J.B., *An Inspector Calls*, 1993. Reprinted by permission of Pearson Education Limited

Cover design by Will Dady

Printed on FSC-accredited papers in the UK by 4edge Limited

ISBN: 978-1-80447-076-3

9 8 7 6 5 4 3 2

ONE WOMAN

CRIME WAVE

'Dad, if you call the police you will never see me again.'

He walked past McDonalds and the smells poured out, eggs and coffee, simple smells. Ludi remembered smells like something from before. Normally he'd be straight in there for an Egg McMuffin but now his stomach heaved. He was walking forwards but pacing back in his mind. Back to last week when his life was just a life. Back five years when she was still a child. His child. Back to today, just this morning, when they found her. In that – whatever that place was, a loony bin. A crazy weird pile of madness with his own daughter at the middle of it all.

Christ almighty, with his own eyes. And that Tara woman going I will make her pay, I will make her pay! It pulled open the wounds. He tried to think back. Was there a link, from this, from now, to back then, to earlier? It hurt too much to go back into the memories. Ludi shook his head. He didn't want to, it still hurt. But now he needed to understand Ashleigh. His own daughter, just this morning, right to his face. 'Dad, if you call the police you will never see me again.'

His mind shook. He had called her phone again and again, first raging then in fear. Where was she now? He thought of those missing child stories on the news, and a memory came, Ashleigh's first school photo. There was nobody to give the extra copies to, they never had no one. But still bought the most expensive set: multiple photos in every size. The whole flat covered in different-sized Ashleighs, all smiling away with her gappy teeth. It's those photos they show on telly when a kid goes missing.

His mouth dried up and felt like his voice had disappeared, he hummed to see if it was still there. The hum died in his throat. He walked by the neon poster on the bus stop, Olympics logo – it was everywhere. *A City Like No Other.* No shit. *Fifty nationalities, the home of the avant-garde and high finance.* This was his home too. This same old road, straight out of the heart of old London. He'd pushed the buggy round these streets, and done countless call outs. Streets that had once been fields, where other men trudged, with other fears that no one knew about.

Where was she? Ludi turned off and took a side road, the other way round over the railway bridge where him and the kids used to watch the trains. The hedges were growing out into the pavement, he let them catch his face. There was the bridge, the sign with the emergency number in case of a crash. Who did you call if your life crashed. There was the usual graffiti and above it in giant letters one painted word HOPE. He'd never really looked at it before.

Hope. The wind pushed a crisp packet along the gutter. He thought he knew his daughter. Then today found out he didn't. That was the worst. And now he was walking around half destroyed and wearing a jacket stuffed with cash. So maybe this was the worst. Maybe this was a whole new worst, only just beginning.

PART ONE

'If we were all responsible for everything that happened to everyone we'd had anything to do with, it would be very awkward, wouldn't it?'

J.B. PRIESTLEY

1

ASHLEIGH ARRIVES

Ashleigh pushed the doorbell and took a quick step back. She stood straight and looked up at the front of the house and the upstairs windows. It was the same house. But not the same. A small front garden with tidy hedges, like a house in an advert. She had never been back. She looked away from the rocking horse in the front window – she didn't want to be peering in when they answered. Guess who's back, she murmured. She took a breath, prepared a minimal smile and looked directly at the centre of the door.

'Hi I'm Tara, and you must be the famous Ashleigh,' Tara smiled widely as she pulled the door all the way open and they looked at each other for a second.

'Come on in!'

'Hi – thanks,' Ashleigh moved past her into the house and felt Tara's eyes skim down and up as she went. Ashleigh had crafted the Perfect Babysitter look: pink sweatshirt and nice jeans, no make-up. Her straight blonde hair was in a loose bun with strands hanging out and she was carrying a school bag on her back.

'Great! Please, take a seat! Make yourself comfortable!'

Ashleigh slipped the bag off as they came to the table, balancing it on her lap as they both sat down.

'I'm told you're the number-one babysitter in the neighbourhood!' Tara's voice was full of exclamation marks and her eyes and mouth were big.

Ashleigh laughed politely. 'Thanks, it's all through school. I'm at Selby High now but my little sister Morgan still goes there, she's in Year Five.'

'OK!'

'So, what year is Betsy in?'

'Betsy's seven now, she's in Year Two.' Tara began describing Betsy's routine. It sounded like she'd covered this a hundred times: sleep regimes, special toys, favourite songs and books, rules on food. Ashleigh nodded thoughtfully, maintaining eye contact.

'She has to have her toys arranged in a special way before she can sleep, just one of those funny things!' Tara stood up as she carried on talking, and dabbed some Touche Éclat under her eyes in the mirror. 'Giles is already putting her down though,' she said. 'She's a good sleeper so you won't have any trouble.'

'Ah OK, that's nice.'

'And it's great that you live so close by. Our nanny Samina wasn't free tonight. She's wonderful but you know – it helps to have backup!' Tara scrabbled in her make-up bag and there was a comfortable pause. 'Do you do school pickups?'

'Yes, I used to collect Morgan but now she does football until Dad gets her, so I'm free most evenings.'

'Good to know! I work in TV,' Tara added breezily, 'but I've recently started writing, I'm working on a screenplay so I often need some extra help.'

'Oh that's so cool!'

Tara smiled as she leant towards the mirror, checked her teeth and shook her hair out of its ponytail. 'And you live in the blocks, just over…?'

'Yes I live in Tanghall,' Ashleigh said, and let the slight pause hang there. Everyone knew those blocks. Ashleigh caught the raised eyebrow in the mirror and the 'haven't you done well' look. She couldn't help herself: 'I used to live here, though!' she said, immediately surprised by having let it out. Ashleigh never usually shared stuff, let alone something like this.

'Excuse me?' Tara was finishing her eyeliner. The fridge buzzed, there was a sound of footsteps upstairs. Ashleigh glanced away, through to the French windows leading out of the kitchen.

'I used to live here,' she went on, 'when this house was flats. We lived upstairs. Before we moved out, it was about five, six years ago?'

'Here, really?' Tara frowned slightly. 'Well isn't that funny. This must be a trip down memory lane for you.' She added one last flick of mascara and blinked at herself in the mirror.

Giles came rumbling down the stairs and into the room, wearing beaten-up Converse, jeans and a hoody.

'She's down at last. Just listening to the CD. Oh, hello!'

His eyes took Ashleigh in with the thrill of enjoying, up close, that sly fresh teenage beauty. When his gaze reached her face she raised her chin very slightly. He looked away and adjusted his watch strap.

'Yes, this is Ashleigh and she used to live here – isn't that sweet,' said Tara, pushing the chair back as she stood up. 'Come on, let's get going or we'll be late. Have you got the car keys?'

A few more goodbyes, then the front door closed and they walked away. Ashleigh listened, tracking the sounds as they left. Finally that was it – they were gone. And there she was, sitting at the kitchen table. They'd been super-friendly.

13

They'd done the cool parent thing of pretending to be on Ashleigh's side: 'Kids eh, they're a nightmare haha.' And she had done the sensible babysitter thing, and looked them straight in the eye, calm.

She always brought her school bag along, filled with books. They loved that, the parents. And she made sure to include science or maths books, because they also loved saying 'Oh, I was terrible at that. Let's have a look, wow, I could never do that. Isn't it cool how girls are doing these subjects nowadays!' and they'd laugh. And Ashleigh would smile modestly. And she'd think – just wait till you get out that door.

She drummed her fingers and then her fingernails on the oak table. A brand new place. And this was not just any place. This would be special, better than the rest. She shut her eyes. This was the best part. When the parents left, here's how it went. First, she spread out her books and pencil case. She opened a page and made a few notes. This should take at least ten minutes because parents generally came crashing back through the door – 'I forgot my keys/phone/wallet' – and there she'd be, phone face-down and pencil poised. Everyone's favourite A-starred angel.

Ashleigh checked the time on her phone. Ten minutes was usually about right. Today she would make herself wait for more than fifteen though. It made it more exciting. She hummed quietly. She'd discovered there was even a name for it: 'deferred gratification'. A delicious name, she thought. Kind of a strong name.

The other thing parents did was send a text once they were on their way. Basically so they didn't feel guilty about leaving their kids with a complete stranger. It helped them feel like they were still in control. It usually went something like *If he wakes up – spare milk in fridge ☺ back around 11.* And Ashleigh would always send a prompt and reassuring reply. And then came that surge of the most powerful joy.

Because they were not in control.

2

TARA ARRIVES

Tara was unusually perky in the car on the way to the dinner party. The other mums were right, she told Giles, this was no ordinary babysitter.

'I mean, the gold hoop earrings are a bit councily, but no accent at all, nothing to rub off on Betsy – not like that au pair with the cheap perfume!'

And they laughed. Giles swept his hands confidently on the steering wheel as they turned into a street full of tall white stucco London houses with massive bay windows.

'Aha – the perfect space!' Giles began to reverse into a parking spot. 'What did you mean she used to live in our house though?'

'It must've been that upstairs tenant who delayed the sale for ages, remember? Oh god, and that old carpet,' Tara said.

'The rhapsody in brown!' said Giles, and they laughed again. They had moved in seven months later when it was all knocked through.

'OK, here we are.'

Tara felt dwarfed by the wide steps leading up to the front door. Inside they hugged and cheek-kissed the hosts, and Tara caught sight of herself in the hall mirror. Her chestnut base with balayage chocolate lowlights gleamed in the halogens. She took a breath and felt good again as they were led downstairs. The dinner party was with some of Giles' old friends from university. They had less interesting jobs than him but much bigger houses, she noted, then smiled her confident smile and scanned the row of faces.

They were sitting along a long oak table with masses of tea-lights down the middle, in a huge basement kitchen with a wine wall.

'Oh yes – lovely, elderflower fizz please,' Tara accepted a glass and laughed. 'I'm the boring one tonight as it's my turn to drive!' As she sat down Tara could see the conversations were already beginning to self-select by gender. She was in sub-prime seating towards the end of the table, with the hosts at the other end. Which was worse: lumping all the men together to bray over each other, or alternating them between buffers of sacrificial women to soak up the shoutiness? She could shout just as well as them, but she was tired, and the lack of wine didn't help.

She gulped in preparation for someone asking about her job. The truth was that since having a baby, the world of TV had closed behind her and pulled down the shutters. She had agonised over whether to add the word 'Mum' to her online profile. Maybe it could unlock access to a working-mum elite. Those ninja-mothers probably didn't boast about being mums though, they were too busy succeeding: 'What – these? Oh they're just some gifted children I popped out between award-winning documentaries. But you'd never know from these abs of steel haha!'

Tara adjusted her ponytail. It wasn't just work – it was the social life that came with it that she craved. She used to be the life and soul. And Betsy was seven years old now but Tara still hadn't regained her party mojo. If anything, it was getting harder. She looked around again, she wasn't near anyone she knew. Giles was up there, three people away. Far enough for her not to be able to join in, but close enough to hear his voice. Look at him, tipping his chair away from the table and stretching his arms out wide. He ran his fingers through his hair. It was messed up to look like someone who didn't care. She knew exactly how much he cared.

She tried to block out the familiar opening lines about his newspaper column.

'Oldest trick in the book,' he was saying. 'Fillet everyone for all the copy you can get, but make sure to give your sharpest putdowns to the wife. That way everyone looks good, isn't that right, Tara,' he shouted down to her. She smiled indulgently and looked down at the Ottolenghi shakshuka and jewel-coloured salads on her plate.

'Yeah, bloody funny,' chimed a guy who worked in private equity.

'We've all been there,' the man on Giles' other side spoke over him. 'You know the competing parents, that school-rage thing you wrote about…'

'Oh that,' Giles rotated like a lighthouse. 'But things have changed. I went to state school' – he paused to let that soak in – 'but these days even that's not enough. Anti-privilege has gone so far the only way to compete is to have had a childhood straight out of the Monty Python four Yorkshiremen sketch.'

The private equity man tried again: 'Eeh, we dreamt of a cardboard box.'

Tara considered his determined pink face and wondered whether a banker would have been a better life partner. They're never there, for starters. Look at him; she thought, conversational antimatter, but probably even his job ranks above being a mum who once worked in TV. She brought her gaze back to the people closer by. She straightened her back and put on an active listening expression, curious yet unjudging, like a therapist.

A pointy woman with baked-looking blonde hair projected in: 'The way it's going the only way into Oxbridge will be to have a disadvantage, never mind top grades – they'll need some kind of mental health problem, or be, you know, *ethnic*.' It was the same conversation taking place, in stereo, to either side of her. Tara sighed, and like a weary tennis spectator returned her gaze from the blonde woman back to Giles' persevering neighbours.

'I for one am sick of being expected to apologise for having gone to a decent school—'

'We're rolling out inclusive recruitment but I keep saying: I just want the best person for the job.'

With a sudden light feeling Tara realised she could throw the same line in both directions at once. She took a sip from her glass, looked both ways and cleared her throat, 'If you add up everyone who's a minority then surely *we're* the endangered ones!'

No. It didn't work – no one heard. The flows continued uninterrupted around her. She stared down at the empty fork in her hand, orphaned in the middle without a claim on either conversation. She picked out a pomegranate seed, chewed it slowly. Wasn't that the food of the underworld? She began to eat her way round the edge of an egg yolk, keeping it intact. Ottolenghi and competitive fury, that's what we enjoy while paying someone else to sit in our house. She reached over and took an olive from a carved wooden dish.

No one had asked about her work. In theory she could still say she worked in television, even though it was only development. Plus the volunteering for No Cuts, the anti-FGM campaign. They came to give an awareness event in school and in the resultant indignation Tara had offered to help out by writing a blog. Female genital mutilation – can you believe these people! Right here in London too, and more common than anyone knows. Cutting little girls only slightly older than Betsy!

She wriggled the olive stone out the side of her mouth but there was nowhere to put it. Her blog had got over two thousand shares though, people were taking notice. But it wasn't enough. The truth was that her professional muscles had atrophied away in a sea of mums' lattes, and no amount of yoga could fix that. So now she was trying to develop the blog into the beginnings of a screenplay. 'How's the "work of art" coming along,' Giles would ask, using actual sarcastic fingers, whenever he saw her on social media.

She put the olive stone on the side of her plate and looked up the table. There he was, three seats along. He drew energy from around him like a flat iPhone brightening into life, charging up from the duller glows on every side. Tara slumped slightly as she became an audience member. Giles was extolling Avenue Road Primary, their local state school, and its melting-pot diversity. All mixed up together like bees in a hive – adorable. But secondary school, no way. Then it had to be private, this way you got the best of both.

Tara had no desire to take part in this exchange. She knew that once people started talking about schools then the tutoring conversation wasn't far behind. It set off a small glow of panic inside her that she and Giles still hadn't solved the problem of Betsy.

'Actually,' the guy next to Giles butted in, 'our neighbours did it the other way round – they sent their girl to state school at the end, for her A levels, and that way she got a lower offer from Durham!'

Right on cue someone mentioned a tutoring service that was tailor-made to make your child appear untutored, because apparently Oxbridge could now spot that a mile off: 'This way they come over as smart but in a raw, original way.'

'Whatever it takes – but my point is,' Giles allowed a theatrical pause, 'diversity's all very well but, you know – I don't want dealers at the school gate.' Another pause. 'Unless I can get my hands on some of the stash too HAHA!'

This rolled all the way down the table on a wave of delighted outrage, sparking a happy consensus that private schools were awash with drugs too, but at least they were likely to be of a better quality. The baked-blonde woman looked over with a 'isn't your husband naughty' smile, and Tara gave a half smile back.

Why hadn't anyone asked about her work? Didn't she even look like someone with a job? She realised she was biting the insides of her cheeks so she tried a calming breath. Out of nowhere her eyes suddenly filled with tears, the candles along the table blurred into a bright mess. She remembered her mindfulness app: look at the pebble, imagine its touch. She'd forgotten to do the pebble today. Her stomach bubbled and made a mournful noise like whale song.

She glanced back at Giles, watched him shake a salad leaf off his fork before restacking it and filling his open mouth. She recalled seeing him through the bathroom door that morning, shaking drops off his penis. Like taking the petrol pump out of the car. She looked away again, returning to the guy on her other side. On the way she prayed her silent dinner party prayer: *Please don't talk about schools – I'll do anything, even house prices, but please please not schools…*

'So we're pretty delighted,' her neighbour beamed. 'Our oldest just got a scholarship!'

3

ASHLEIGH EXPLORES

Ashleigh stood up and took a deep breath. She quietly replaced the chair under the table and walked to the fridge. She stood and looked. The usual layers of school letters and babyish drawings covered its door. That's what they want everyone to see. It's what's behind that counts. The huge silver door swung back. Here we go, as easy as if they'd left their bank statements open on the table. She was guessing M&S ready meals, farmer's market stuff, no Tesco and definitely no Supervalu.

Woah, but these guys. Two bottles of champagne, not Prosecco. Ready-picked pomegranate seeds like a bowl of rubies, and fresh herbs. Italian water. Brown mushrooms in a cardboard tray. Soya milk. Greek yoghurt with Greek writing on, and different coloured olives in a jar. Some butter that wasn't from a supermarket. She used to like the big brands but now she knew that not having any brand at all was even posher. No ready meals – not even in the freezer. There was a weird-looking cheese wrapped in paper inside the door. She sniffed it and put it back.

Ashleigh always started with the kitchen, inch by inch, shelf by shelf. She examined everything they ate, she assessed and catalogued each discovery, careful to note and memorise anything unfamiliar. She had trained herself to take her time, steadily, turning items over, unwrapping, looking behind, seeing every angle. She would eventually move on to each and every thing they stored. But she started here with the daily stuff: fresh foods, snacks and breakfast.

Breakfast was gross: grey oats, dusty muesli. But apart from breakfast, everything was better for rich people. Even their sugar. Who knew that sugar could be so different. She took a pinch and spread it out on the marble counter. Like grains of sand from a tropical beach – each particle was irregular, distinct. Bigger than normal sugar. She separated out one crystal, rolled it between her finger and thumb, then licked it. It tasted golden, almost smoky. She swept the leftover grains into her pencil case. She would compare them to the stuff her dad loaded into his mugs of tea.

She liked moving things around and she'd notice herself remembering how to set everything back precisely afterwards. Sometimes she'd even do a few different moves in a row to test herself. Then she'd have to do them backwards and in reverse order. She'd stand on a chair or even climb along the kitchen surfaces, reaching up for the high shelves. She could recite the geometry of her moves and climbs. And the higher she reached, the more unlikely the discoveries.

To date, her top-shelf favourites were a tin of tongue – tongue! – four years out of date, and a packet of lentils. The lentils on their own weren't interesting until you compared them to what was in the fridge. Like she'd learnt in history: context was everything. When you looked in their fridge and saw only a stack of mid-range ready meals, then you knew for sure this unopened lentil tragedy was some kind of promise gone wrong. They would never see the light of day. Every time she babysat at Charlotte's place she revisited them, the lentils of lost dreams, to enjoy the failure.

Yes the backs of the cupboards revealed as much if not more than the fridge. They showed the hidden hopes. Back here was where she found the context, the deeper history. Mr Stokes would love this – she wished she could do an essay about it. He was the best teacher. Today they did fascism and its distinguishing features including scapegoats, propaganda, and the refusal to tolerate free inquiry. Ashleigh collected phrases like this, repeating them inside her head. Then later she'd practise them out loud when she was alone:

'But surely its distinguishing feature is its refusal to tolerate free inquiry?'

I'll give you a free inquiry, she laughed quietly. She reached up higher. These shelves were like a wish-list zone. Probably inspired by a TV show, foods that seemed a good idea at the time but would never happen. They were people's more successful, healthy vision of their own lives. Unopened spices, experimental noodles, unrecognisable kitchen implements. That bag labelled Authentic Organic Chapatti Flour. As if.

Anyway there was nothing like that here. This was the most impressive kitchen she'd ever done. The cupboards weren't messy or piled high, they were organised. More than organised, they were – what was the word? Curated. It was more like those shops around Bond Street, the kind so fancy they hardly sell anything. Like one pair of shoes in a single spotlight. No top-shelf shame round here.

Le Creuset. Bitossi. Liberty London. And their cups were all small. No supersized mugs with slogans or cartoons on. None of that. She would keep looking. Everyone has something to hide, and she always kept going until she found it. Higher shelves were the obvious place where parents stashed their treats. Mostly biscuits and crisps, and usually behind big things like pasta or flour. One day she'd alert the children she babysat to this deception. The 'unacceptable' booze also lived up here. Cheap quarter-bottles of whiskey and vodka from Londis, next to boxes of instant cake: simply add one egg.

Once she had uncovered a priceless trove. It was one of her other homes – Stacey's kids. A regular Weetabix box, but by chance she squeezed it, and it felt wrong. Inside was a folded-over bag pushed deep down. Froot Loops with Marshmallows. With a rush of delight Ashleigh realised that Stacey probably had an eating disorder, and sure enough she eventually found, in the bottom of the lowest fridge department, inside a salad bag with another salad bag on top, a giant Galaxy bar. It had actual teeth marks in it. She uncovered facts, checked her theories and proved them, growing her knowledge of their lives. Houses and flats, posh and normal. Certain truths applied everywhere, that was the best part. They all wanted to show some things and hide others.

This kitchen was the back half of a much larger knocked-through room, with the fireplace, the TV and the sofa, the desk with a computer and a monitor screen. There was a tall lamp at the side of two framed paintings that really were paintings and not photos of a painting. She picked up a stack of papers lying on top of the printer and flicked through: maths pages and word searches, a few school letters. She ran a finger over the controls. She always had to print out her own work at school or in the library.

The shelves were bookended by shiny houseplants. Ashleigh touched a leaf, admiring its high gloss. She poked the soil to see if it was fake. It wasn't. Once she'd had her own plant, a tiny rosebush from the garage shop. It lived on the kitchen windowsill in their flat. One day she saw a couple of greenflies. The next time she looked the bush was covered, smothered by tiny creatures. Her dad swore and threw the whole thing in the rubbish. But Ashleigh didn't hate them. They hadn't missed a single leaf, stem or bud. That was how to do it. Thorough.

From here in the kitchen heartlands she would move outwards, uncovering every secret, every intimate area of the home, expanding. She knew more than they did. It gave her a towering feeling that grew each time, it got better and better, and so did she. Sometimes she could feel her own pulse. Ashleigh was proud not to miss one centimetre of any of the homes she worked in. She always found what she wanted, in the end.

4

TARA ENDURES

'Are the Olympics too expensive? Maybe,' Giles paused, 'but I'm not complaining about the ladies' beach volleyball!'

The woman whose house this was moved around the table, reaching between people to gather up the plates. None of the men helped, Tara noticed, and she was about to offer when she realised it was patriarchal and decided against.

'No one fancies skinny women, you know,' Giles went on. 'Isn't the ultimate triumph of feminism that women starve themselves not to please men but to please each other?'

There was a ripple of nervous laughter and several bony women at the table avoided each other's gaze. Tara looked away from him.

'But seriously, women are taking over now – and about time too. My boss is a woman. At work and at home haha.' He raised his glass. 'I'm a feminist too. Here's to women!'

She tuned back into the blonde woman's monologue, which continued without hesitation as the creamy lime and coconut syllabubs landed, concluding:

'I saw this thing on Indian street children and the caste system – it was simply unbearable, the way they treat them. I just feel like, having kids, as a mum, it literally connects us to the world, it makes me care more, you know?'

'I don't agree,' Tara finally got a word in, her face ached with the strain of passive listening.

'Having kids makes you care about your own kids. Not other people's! And as for caste systems, well, our country is run by Etonians, so…?'

Tara saw one of the woman's eyes flinch – clearly this was someone with a centuries-long connection to Eton.

'Wow,' she continued less emphatically. 'Did she say this syllabub was vegan?'

They both looked away. Tara sat back again. It would be less effort just to allow the evening to wash over her.

The mood of the table took a sudden turn for the optimistic. It was agreed that the era of 'isms' was finally over; for all people kept going on about social mobility it was clear that humans had basically cracked it. Even disabled people had got their own Olympics, and why not, it was the best time to be alive, and the best place too. Never mind Great Britain, this was Great London!

Giles then launched into the UK Independence Party clowns – they'd put the wrong name on their mayoral ballot papers, 'But their leader blamed the voters, saying they didn't understand – how never to get another vote again!'

'He's on the news all the time, though, so someone must like him!'

'Only morons. And northerners,' Giles boomed. 'It's nothing more than a suburban nostalgia kick, a blast from the past.'

Such conviction – it was so solid and dependable, Tara admired it in a way. She remembered that dinner where Giles sat near someone from Thailand, and explained that nation's politics to her on the basis of his holiday there six years earlier. It wasn't the information itself but the sharing of it that seemed to give him such a hard-on. She sighed and looked around. The blonde woman had now co-opted someone else and was laughing hard.

She refilled her glass with water this time, she'd finished the elderflower fizz. She turned and caught the eye of the man on her other side. She smiled generously and he introduced himself as Alex, a lawyer. He was in the middle of a story about the time the Australian government flew him in to advise on tax reform. He pushed back from the table to include her, expanding as he spoke. She couldn't tell whether she was supposed to be pleased or appalled by the story so she looked at his torso and imagined him reaching orgasm. The thought coincided with her last spoonful of the watery bit at the bottom of the syllabub. She frowned.

Alex the lawyer carried on talking. He was now this end of the table's counterweight to Giles. What did these men do when there weren't any women to listen to them, she wondered. She eyed his shoes, they were the slip-on kind, with a golden buckle! Who wears those? Probably Berlusconi. And men who pay for sex. He went on to broadcast a series of unrelated facts such as aphids contain their own grandchildren, and his father was 100% self-made. Tara's face continued to smile while she pondered the lack of names for men who pay for sex, when there are so many for women who sell it.

The topic of childcare moved down from the other end of the table, providing a welcome change of voices as well as a showcase for open-mindedness. Someone mentioned their nanny who was 'from Africa'. This was teaching the children not to be racist, 'But our cleaner's Latvian and she is racist, which is crazy really!' This was instantly bested by someone who had a 'manny, a male nanny'. Everyone stopped and tuned in.

'We're totally subverting gender stereotypes – men can be just as caring, and Dolly and Jess are learning to play football too.'

Everyone chuckled fondly. Giles didn't chuckle. He couldn't help himself: 'We've got a Muzzer.'

'A what?'

Tara shot him a warning glance. 'A Muslim. I mean she doesn't wear one of those scarf things but she's a proper Muslim, her family's actually from Iran. I mean Iraq. So when it comes to being radicalised our kids will totally have the edge: *Allahu Akbar!*'

It was a joke too far, Tara felt, but there was definitely something off about her. She leant an elbow on the table, pondering the subject of their nanny Samina. She was too chatty. And what about that time Tara jokingly said, 'Oh god, there's so much booze in the fridge – what must you think of us?' And she had simply agreed: 'Yes, it is a lot.' And Tara's laughter had been left hanging. Ever since then, Tara had felt judged. By her own nanny!

In any case they'd recently talked about Samina being too expensive. Tara ate a cantuccio biscuit, hearing the crunching and grinding inside her own head. Coffee and tea came and went. She had another cantuccio biscuit. As a child she'd been taught to chew her food twenty times. She chewed slowly and purposefully, as if she was carefully considering the flavours within each bite, covering up the fact that she had no one to talk to. Alex the lawyer was deeply engrossed in the pointy blonde who was now laughing her head off.

Probably no one knew that she used to work in TV. They obviously thought she was just a mum. As she chewed and swallowed and chewed again Tara found she couldn't summon up the slightest glimmer of energy to join in on whether box sets or social media was the biggest threat to reading books. On how much of a crackhead Whitney Houston had been. On whether Obama would get re-elected. She nibbled the side of her thumbnail. Whoosh, whoosh, the conversations swept around her. She was dinner-party roadkill, lying squashed flat at the side of the road as the traffic passed by. And of course Giles was still holding court. She looked over and saw he was now starting to roll a joint. Typical, thought Tara, he's at the cool end and I'm here in Etonian isolation.

'I went to state school,' she heard Giles repeating, 'and here's the thing: I still know where to get top blow!'

This was a bit of a risk – they might not like this. Tara looked at his neighbours to see if they were shocked.

'I just call my man up any time and get what I need. He's over in the estate, those Tanghall blocks,' he went on, 'and you know it's good to support local business haha.'

She needn't have worried. Everyone laughed about buying local, and Giles was now a hero of the multiverse. What would it be like to have a shy husband, she wondered. She entertained a brief cost-benefit analysis of his job: it didn't pay well, but it was cool. Their kitchen wasn't big enough to seat twelve people, but everyone always wanted to talk to Giles. She supposed this was to her advantage.

Her mind flicked back to Hot Trainer, the guy who got her back into shape when Betsy first started nursery. All the mums lusted after him, his white teeth, his delicious Brazilian limbs, and she revelled in their nickname for him. She couldn't suppress a slow smile. It had made her feel so good. Obviously she wouldn't want to be married to him, and she had long since shut him out of her thoughts. But he still got into her dreams, the dream of pulling him to her, riding him hard.

Tara shuffled in her seat. The same dreams that haunted her sticky nights, the ones where she woke up burning.

Was it Giles' fault that she felt like she was in decline, somehow less of herself than she used to be? It was certainly his fault that he hoovered up all the oxygen in the room at every single opportunity. He was the dry nightmare to her wet dream. In decline – aged only forty-two! Why couldn't her life be ablaze, be the way that music used to make her feel, when everything was a soundtrack, when it felt like she was in a movie about her own brilliant life, when she was free.

But no. Instead of that, here she was. Sitting, chewing, sinking, her arse gradually spreading outwards on the chair, the chewed-up food chugging down into her digestive system on its tiresome, dutiful journey, with all these stretching duplicitous faces and the endless buzzing waffling braying noises around her. She paused, balancing her fork on the end of her finger, it hovered there. Her eyes fixed on the tips of its silver tines, then she let her gaze go out of focus.

Was it so hard to talk about real and truthful things? Why not have a conversation about the last time they had a quivering sex dream about someone massively inappropriate? Tara could feel her pulse. Hot Trainer's shiny torso flashed into her mind. Why not just be honest? Just say I hate you, I wish for nothing more than your failure! I hope you get divorced so we can all talk about it! She let the fork drop, filled with a bursting urge to stand up, to explode, to rip down her knickers and show them her pussy. Her perfect well-kept pussy – yes she used that word, so what – to shout out loud: 'LOOK! Can you see me now?'

'Erm, could you pass the soya milk?' The blonde woman was looking at her.

Tara jumped. 'Oh sorry. Yes. Here.'

5

ASHLEIGH OBSERVES

This house was different, though. Ashleigh sat down on the sofa then stood up again. This house contained part of her childhood, her own self, inside these walls. She heard her earlier comment, 'I used to live here,' and Tara's reply echoed, 'This must be a trip down memory lane for you.'

She walked slowly around the room, anticipating a sudden new memory or some kind of shivery feeling. None came. She didn't recognise anything. But she was here first, before Tara! Her family, in the upstairs flat. Dad, Morgan – just a baby. And Mum… Back when her family was whole.

She returned to the fridge and ruffled through the pictures and papers that were held there with magnets. There: a bright felt-tip drawing of a wonky person with big hands coming straight off its body and unmatching eyes. Below it said I Love My Mummy in babyish writing, some of the letters were backwards. Ashleigh took it off the fridge door and held it in both hands, her eyes glittering.

She left the room and went upstairs, lightly touching the paintwork all the way up. She paused at the top then pushed open the door into what had once been their kitchen. The narrator voice came up in her head: Guess who's back. It wasn't as fun as usual though. She looked down at her feet in the doorway. How long ago? Her long-ago family. What had there been, here in this space? The lino floor, a repeating red and black pattern. A small table, three chairs. That kettle with the ringing whistle where the steam came out. The cooker where the milk boiled over.

She took one step inside. It had been here, right here – that a marble had rolled under the cooker and she tried to reach under and get it back. It was the best marble, the only one with no colour streak but just silver bubbles. It was the special one and she had loved it. Reaching under, cheek pressed to the floor, underneath she had spied the edge of the lino curling up. No one else knew that the lino didn't reach the wall. That felt important at the time. She remembered liking it that no one else knew. But she never got her marble back.

Ashleigh stood, staring. What else was there? 'Memory lane.' Their family kitchen was now a spare room with light grey curtains, white walls, books, and dark wooden furniture that looked antique. How could the same space become not the same space? She looked at where the cooker once stood. She used to make breakfast, toast under the grill. Sometimes it burnt. She remembered the whoosh of tiny blue flames fanning across. Morgan crying.

Maybe the marble was still here, underneath, deep in dust, gleaming below the floorboards. And look – she was here too. I was here first! She moved to the window. It was still light out and she could see the trees and the garden fence. She waited. There had to be something she could get from this. Not from objects, but from inside her own head. She squinted until her face ached but couldn't force the memories to come. Only the toast, burnt toast – was that it? Some shouting memories. Her breath steamed up the glass of the window pane as she leant, still looking out.

The leaving had been bad, so bad, with Dad loading everything into Steve's van. Shouting. She remembered they put their stuff into boxes from Londis, and the banana box broke on the stairs. And shouting, always shouting. She bet these parents, with their fucking magical sugar and their walls full of books, she bet they never shouted like that. Probably never burnt the toast. She drew a miniature sad face into the patch of mist on the glass then wiped it away with her sleeve.

Ashleigh turned her back to the window and returned to the moment. Time to move on. She moved silently to the child's door and listened outside. Nothing. She'd check on her later. Onwards to the bathroom – this would deliver. The door swung open, two enormous fluffy towelling robes were hanging on the back. White Company, of course. Their pockets were empty. No end of thick towels hung on a shiny rail that was hot to the touch. The surfaces were marble, the cupboard doors were shiny, the mirror was huge.

She sighed. She pulled down her jeans and knickers and sat down on the toilet to pee. She was feeling weirdly flat. Tonight wasn't meeting her expectations. 'Dismayed, despondent,' she pronounced out loud, 'when I should be fully mayed and pondent.' She reached for the toilet roll and frowned. It was surprisingly familiar: regular plain white instead of luxury quilted.

Still sitting, she reached and checked the toilet brush, lifting it from the discreet shelter sculpted like an alien pod. Often they were surprisingly shitty. Not this one. Inside was no hidden puddle of brown fluid, not so much as a single pube on the brush. She held it up and rotated it, slowly, observing it from every angle. She replaced it, then in one swift move she wiped, zipped up and flushed. There had to be a flaw here somewhere, and she would find it and that would cheer her up.

'OK, let's get to work.'

The sink area was immaculate, divided along a his and hers pattern. She opened a Clarins Day Cream, making sure her finger scoop followed the previous finger's precise route. She dabbed on some La Mer Eye Balm Intense and pulled out the extending magnified mirror to admire herself from the side. There was some fake tan she might do later too. She held up a small perfume bottle with a squat gold lid. Maison Francis Kurkdjian, what? She opened it. It smelt like wet soil. She grimaced and put it back.

Ashleigh started opening the drawers first to the left and then the right of the sink unit, and worked her way down, front to back, scrupulously replacing each item with absolute precision.

The drawers followed the same his and hers pattern as the sink. She knew which way the labels faced – everything. That's how good she was. She tingled with the sensation of her own skills. She was electric.

Here we go – now we're getting somewhere. She held up a bottle of Davines NaturalTech Energizing Shampoo. Stimulates circulation using caffeine phytoceuticals. Why of course it does. So it was the hair. Shelf after shelf of hair products – Shu Uemura Frame Wax, Kiehl's Creme with Silk Groom, Phyto Wet Gel, Vitamin-Surge Follicular Boost, trimmers, cutters, tweezers and appliances she'd never seen before. The funny thing was he looked so trampy, she never would have predicted this stash.

Then Tara's side. Not much make-up but a lot of skincare. Some of the free samples weren't even opened. Then, at the back of the bottom drawer was a clear plastic Ziploc bag inside a Clarins bag. She lifted it out and opened it under the bright lights. It contained what looked like a bunch of dirty dry twigs. She opened and sniffed them cautiously, took one of the grey-brown lumps out and rolled it in her fingertips. Absolutely no idea. This went on the list for further investigation. She'd be back.

Up a level, in a corner cupboard above the toilet, was a large bottle of Deflatine. 'Eases the symptoms caused by trapped wind.' What a pig. She read the side, scanning the active ingredients and the words 'unhappy tummy'. He did look a bit gassy now she thought of it. She shook the bottle and felt its liquid movement, imagined it sliding down inside his farty guts. Maybe he was going to guzzle it tonight. She unscrewed the lid, lightly touched her tongue to the rim and pulled a face in the mirror.

She liked to watch herself do it. This was the best part about the bathrooms, ones like this with bright lights and generous mirrors. *Who are these people!* She would hold things up to her reflection with a quizzical or sarcastic look, pretending to be on TV. The imaginary audience was all on her side, willing her on, applauding and mouthing ohmygod; close-ups on faces laughing out of control.

Last of all, the small swing-lid bin next to the sink. She hummed as she bent down, removed the top and lifted out the inside container. She reached inside, moving efficiently like a surgeon, removing each item, one at a time, spreading them out in lines across the floor as exhibits.

Item One: Folded wax strip with hairs in. Pubic hairs. She unfolded it and looked more closely. The hairs were darker than her own. It was impossible to assess their relative curliness as each one was pressed flat, trapped in its see-through strip. The waxy preservation had a distorting effect that reminded her of something.

Ashleigh sat on her heels as her mind flew back to a long-ago school museum trip, to a display of some pickled babies in a jar, looking, apart from the greyness, just like sleeping babies. The teachers were caught out, unsure whether it was OK for their Year Fours to rush around squealing at human remains. The kids were herded away and instructed to draw an elephant's tooth instead.

That same weekend Ashleigh had diverted from her usual library trips. She went back on her own, back to the museum to visit them, the preserved quadruplets from 1876. It wasn't disgusting or even sad. It was amazing. They were labelled as homo sapiens. Knowing man. And if she knew about them then surely she was homo sapiens sapiens, because she knew more.

Old memories made her life feel long though, Ashleigh moved off her heels and back on to her knees. She liked it when life moved forwards. She cleared her throat. There was work to be done. She ignored the tangled nests of dental floss and scrumpled damp tissues, and passed over a handful of empty plastic tampon wrappers and some orangey-tipped used cotton buds. Normal people would be disgusted by this. But not her. Nothing was gross if you thought about it scientifically.

Item Two: Rolled-up sanitary towel, blood. Neatly wrapped in toilet roll. It was surprisingly heavy, cold now, but recently must have been warm, body temperature. Like a brand new corpse. Ashleigh had never seen a dead person but she wondered how long it took to be fully dead, how slowly they cooled down right to the centre. It was strange that this had been warm recently, warm but not alive. She unrolled it. Wow, heavy flow. Chunks. It was so animal, so completely unlike Tara putting on her make-up in the mirror that evening.

Some people thought that periods and shit and things like that were dirty, but Ashleigh found it the opposite. She'd never tell anyone, because they wouldn't understand, but for her these things were the most honest. Like blushing. And smells. They were just as possible to read as a book, in a way. These things were like the honesty of people's bodies, the ultimate give-away, the physical truth. They made everyone the same.

The pain of Ashleigh's own first period was the lack of privacy. She tried to shut down an unwanted flashback to her sister bursting into their cramped bathroom, damp towels on the floor, the door not closing properly, eyes watering, knickers round her knees, painfully struggling with a tampon while Morgan shouted through the crack, 'Ashy, what you doing to your noo-noo, Ashy? Your bum's having a nosebleed!'

She shook her head. There were no other items of interest in here. She put everything back into the bin, all exactly correct in its apparently carelessly discarded state, and stood up. She sighed with contentment, methodically washing her hands. Doing this was how she felt most at home, and most like her real self. More than in her actual life and self and home, which all felt accidental. This, this was no accident – she was making it happen. Home isn't where the heart is – she could almost feel the lightbulb of this thought – home is where I'm in control.

And even better, this really was her home, or at least it had been once. Ashleigh came out of the bathroom and stopped in the hall. But... what? She stood. That specialness made her want to go deeper, to discover something more, to call up ideas that didn't come from the things in a bin or a drawer or on a shelf.

There were ghosts right here in this house, of the home that it had been before, and of her old life. Her memories were still here, whether she wanted them or not. Here where she'd left them. Was anything left? She had slept right here, she paused outside a bedroom door. There was a pink wooden B with painted golden stars on the door, so she knew it was the right one. Ashleigh had been small and sleepy right here too, just like the kid asleep inside here now. She must be about the same size. This girl who had taken her place. It was late enough now to check in on her.

She touched the door handle. Holding her breath slightly, she carefully turned it and slowly pushed the door open. It didn't creak, it just moved softly over the carpet. A small night-light stood on the floor, throwing shadows up the walls. The light from the open door caught the slight movement of a mobile, dangling monkeys reaching their hands out to each other and slowly circling overhead. A CD was still playing quietly: *Baby Genius: Mozart*. The books and toys were all tidy on the shelves. The thick patterned curtains were pulled tightly shut.

In a small bed against the wall was the curled-up shape of Betsy. The air was thick with her breath and warm babyish smells. Ashleigh could tell she was fast asleep, this was good. Sometimes with the heavy sleepers she liked to think of them as being on her team, helping her out like a little gang. But then she reminded herself that they would almost certainly end up just like their parents. Well, she wouldn't be doing that. A while longer she stood in the doorway, her shadow falling into the room across the yellow and orange wool rug.

6

LUDI HAS A SIT DOWN

Ludi often dropped back home between jobs – a nice moment for a sit down or if it was closer for lunch he could make some toast. Perks of being your own boss. And summers were quieter than winter, so you've got to enjoy that while it lasts. He was back home just before four, when usually the place was still empty. It was good, it felt bigger when no one was there. He thought about bringing his gear up, it was still down in the van, and not taking any more calls for the day.

Then he saw Ashleigh's jacket on the chair. He paused: there was no noise – the place was silent.

'Ash?' he called.

No answer. He looked over at the bedroom door and it was slightly open. He went over, pushed it open and stuck his head round. And there she was – he started slightly.

'Gave me a shock!' he said.

Ashleigh was sat reading a book, up on the top bunk. Underneath her was Morgan's bed, scattered with Gogos and Match Attax.

'Doing homework?' He stood in the doorway.

She looked down at him. 'Yeah.'

'Nice with Morgan out, isn't it. You still going round Nicky's to do your reading?'

Nicky was their neighbour back on the old street where they lived before. Proper old gentleman. When they left, Nicky said he was sorry about them moving out, and did Ashleigh want his spare garage room for doing her homework – they make the kids work so hard nowadays. Ludi could hardly speak when Nicky said that. And he never expected Ashleigh to take the offer up but she called it her homework club and who could argue with that.

'Sometimes.'

'I saw him the other day – that's what reminded me,' he spoke softly, like talking to a shy animal. 'Good old Nicky.' Ludi knew his time was running out if he couldn't think of anything else to say.

She looked down at her book and back up again. 'What do you want, Dad?'

'Nothing, love. Just want you to know, I'm proud. The way you work, it's just… it's—'

'OK.'

'Oh, and Nicky was asking how you were – said to say hello.'

'Dad…'

'Yes!'

'Oh, nothing.'

'What?'

'Nothing!' She raised her eyebrows in that way that asked, Why are you still here?

'OK, see you later then. And yes, I'll shut the door!'

Ludi backed away and stood outside the door. He crept away for a few steps then imagined her laughing at him trying to creep, so he walked loudly into the kitchen area and slammed the kettle on. At least when they fought – at least then she noticed his existence. Truth was, he missed being needed. He looked at the kettle as it started to make its noises. Couldn't she need me, just a little bit? Being needed was who he was – it had been his main self, for longer than he could remember. What was he supposed to do if that wasn't his self any more?

He took two mugs off the shelf then stopped and put one back. He would make his own and not offer her one. He might as well get used to it. She was so distant lately. Things were tense and weird, almost as bad as the old days. He'd caught himself getting flashbacks, when Ashleigh got angry, to her mum. And it gave him the fear. He'd always had that fear, that they would take after her, was it in their blood? Thank god for little Morgan, still his little one, still years off turning into a nightmare woman-creature.

The kettle boiled and clicked off and he put a teabag in the mug and poured the boiling water over. It calmed him down. He squeezed the bag out, in the sink, milk out the fridge. He could do this in his sleep. He got a spoon. The sugar tin was nearly empty. There were brown lumps in the white sugar, drips of old tea gone solid. He pressed one with a spoon – it was rock hard. He chiselled it off and put in his mug then added another spoonful. And a bit more. He stirred. That was better. He went over and sat down, sighed and leant back into the sofa.

He took a sip and looked over at the bedroom door again. He thought back to when Ashleigh was small, it made his chest ache. He thought about how he would carry her, lift her up high. That time she got clonked by a swing in the park and he carried her all the way home. When she fell over, he would hold her on his knee, and say it was OK. He'd tell her it was all OK, and in those days it was.

Everything's OK, he'd say, and hold her, it's OK. And that one time she stopped crying and out of the blue she grinned up at him like some mad pixie and went, 'Uh, Dad, I think I can do a lot better than OK!'

And he'd cracked up. They both cracked right up. Who says that? With her little face. Who the hell says *I think I can do a lot better than OK* – like some kind of tiny miniature headmistress, for god's sake. Ludi laughed into his mug. Always one step ahead, that girl. They used to joke about it: how are you today? I'm a lot better than OK, thank you. Oh we're all a lot better than OK. He drank more tea.

These days he wouldn't dream of trying to joke with her. It wasn't just teenage tantrums or sulking, it felt more like a break-up. And there was that huge fight between the girls last year. Was that normal for girls though? He never got to the bottom of it – all he knew was it was about that stupid apple. Ever since then, Ashleigh was always out. Wouldn't eat with them. Always out, or babysitting. Or in a book just ignoring them. Turning her nose up at them.

Was it this hard for mums? That time Ashleigh made him go and buy tampons. The woman in Boots asking 'Applicator or no applicator?' – what in Christ's name? Even his little Morgan, when he called her his princess, said princesses were lame and she wanted to be a kickboxer. But who could he talk to? Ages since he'd been to the pub. He'd got bored of Steve and that lot, going on about foreign workers, and even worse teasing him about whether Ashleigh had any fit mates.

Once he threatened to ground Ashleigh. She said fine: she'd cancel her babysitting and tell them her dad wouldn't allow it. He backed down, muttering well fine go out then and good riddance. And she laughed, bad riddance more like! And he didn't know what that meant. Afterwards it took him ages to shake off the lowness. He wasn't good enough to be Ashleigh's dad. All her jobs, her independence, he knew he should be proud. Most teenagers never stop nagging for cash, he knew that. But she made him feel proud and useless at the same time. That girl will go far, people would say. Far away from me, he'd think.

He drained the last of his tea. He'd go down and empty the van, you couldn't leave anything lying about these days. He put his cup down on the floor. Wasn't Ash always a bit like that, though? The whole secretive thing started when she was little, she used to hide stuff in weird places and go mental if anyone found it. That was when the apple thing started. She kept it in a sock under her pillow, all dried up. He'd found it and threw it out. She screamed so hard she got a nosebleed, tipped out all the rubbish everywhere to get it back. Said it was her mum's. As if an apple could last that long.

7

ASHLEIGH THROWS HER
CARAMEL LATTE

'It'll be good for you, Ashleigh.' Inside her head she mimicked her teacher's voice, 'Make some friends, Ashleigh!' Ms Hay had persuaded her to attend something called an Enrichment Session at the private school up the hill. This was their term for taking in a bunch of local school kids, showing them the infinity lawns and graciously endowing them with half a day's tuition.

'Obviously they only do it to keep their charitable status, but it'll boost your studies,' Ms Hay urged. 'And apparently their lunch buffet is something else!'

Ashleigh was at the back of the group, inside an entrance hall straight out of Hogwarts. She looked up at the tops of the stained-glass windows and wondered what it would be like to wander through here every day, and for that to be normal. She hadn't forgotten that mysterious filtration process at the end of primary school. The gradual dawning that certain kids were destined to go off to a magic land of wearing blazers and carrying around musical instruments and huge PE kits. And now she was here among them, in a hall with portraits and trophies along the walls, and sports fields extending in every direction.

'Hello! I'm Mrs Johnson!' The teacher was older than most of Ashleigh's teachers, with an eager face and thin brown hair. Ashleigh spied on her ankles as she came round passing out laminated name-tags on a safety pin. She was wearing tights under her trousers and clumpy black leather shoes. A large green and red bead necklace hung outside a shirt collar that emerged from her woolly jumper.

Ashleigh was the only one from Selby High; the rest were from other schools so at least she didn't have to talk to anyone. She was tired, almost dizzy. She had hardly slept since the night in Tara's house two days ago. No peace at home with her dad bursting in every minute. Even when she was reading her mind wouldn't settle down. The floor was as shiny as glass and nearby on the reception desk was a golden trophy of tiny person on a horse. She wanted urgently, burningly, to take it, but Mrs Johnson never took her eye off them for a second.

'Welcome to Hillgate School!' she announced, now everyone had been labelled. 'You've all been hand-picked for this special visit, as the very brightest from your schools, so don't be intimidated,' she chuckled. 'I'm sure we're all going to learn a lot today!' Ashleigh didn't look at anyone else. She was beginning to regret signing up to be Enriched. 'But first of all,' Mrs Johnson carried on, 'let's get started with a few little ice-breakers!'

Ashleigh got through the next half hour with the careful application of one-word answers, clenched teeth, and no eye contact. Ice-breakers? In her mind, ice was the only thing keeping these idiots away from her and no amount of walking on upturned tin cans with strings attached was going to change that. Breaking the ice – no fucking way. It was her life's mission to maintain the permafrost and keep people out of her business. Even her own sister, ever since that fight.

Ashleigh silently congratulated herself that her ice remained firmly unbroken.

Once that was over they had a maths masterclass interspersed with quick-fire presentations on resilience and growth mindsets. Mrs Johnson's face seemed to be straining with optimism versus the desire not to intimidate these economically disadvantaged youngsters. Ashleigh finished the exercises, neatly showing her working, and folded her arms. It was all below her level, obviously. But Mrs Johnson was still expanding the others' growth mindsets so she took her book out of her bag and read until it was time to go to the canteen for lunch.

She and the other 'very brightest' weirdos were shown to a corner table. Ashleigh ignored them. They unpacked their own lunches, too shy to approach the various counters of gleaming food, and sat in silence. Ashleigh glanced around and with a stab of horror she recognised someone on the next table. Swishing her shiny straight hair, in the middle of a group of other girls with shiny straight hair. A girl from her primary school, one of those who'd gone off to Blazer Land with all their violins and tennis racquets. There she sat, eating sushi. With chopsticks. *Of course* with chopsticks.

Ashleigh looked side to side with a rising feeling of panic. Her cheese sandwich, white crusts, still hovered in her hand. If it could've spoken it would've screamed Get out. Her insides sloshed like a washing machine. She placed the sandwich on to the centre of the plate in front of her. The cutlery shone around it like a frame. She would slip that silvery spoon into her pocket and slide out through those huge iron gates, and away, all the way, back down the hill to her real life.

'Ashleigh? Ashleigh! OHMYGOD is it you − it is you! Oh my god what are you doing here!'

The girl had materialised right at Ashleigh's side and was now standing over her. Ashleigh raised her head and then her eyes.

'Hello, Eliza.'

Then Ashleigh closed her mouth and didn't say anything else. Neither did Eliza. Ashleigh looked down. Eliza opened her hands and addressed the table at large, 'Can you believe we were at primary school together. Weren't we! I haven't seen you in, like, ages!'

'Mm.'

Ashleigh's neck was burning. The cheese sandwich lay on its plate in front of her. But one of the corners had no cheese in it, it was just bread.

'Oh, OK,' Eliza gave an exaggerated smile and swung her hair, 'I'd better leave you with your...' – she looked round the table as the smile fell off – 'friends.'

Two hours and fifteen minutes later Ashleigh was still raging inside when Mrs Johnson showed them back to the iron gates. But she had kept herself contained. And as she walked down the hill she imagined herself altering states, arranging her mind into a different mood, creating a different self. Oxygen was entering her body. And she would treat herself to a caramel latte. She deserved it.

She paid, collected her extravagant drink and went over to the counter to top up. The milk jug was empty and she turned back. 'Excuse me – there's no milk?'

A tall man in a suit was near her, he turned and spoke quietly down into her face. 'Milk this,' he said, pretending to unzip his trousers.

Ashleigh rushed outside. Her breath got faster; her mouth was locked tight. She hurried without blinking for a whole block. Two breaths in, three breaths out. Again. Again. Then

she turned the corner and threw her caramel latte into someone's front garden, where it violently exploded. The brown
liquid spread wide as she prevented a sob, pushed her hair
back from her face and moved onwards. All of this — it was
an exercise in self control. All the way back down to her
old primary school, where she slowed as she approached the
school gate queue. If she was in control, then she was still
winning. Today she had to collect one of Stacey's kids, Hugo
in Year Six. She kept her eyes down. She could still get her
calmness back. Her professional self.

'Hi there,' someone next to her chatted as the queue
moved into the playground. Ashleigh gave a tight smile
but managed to avoid eye contact. She moved to the side,
pulled her book out of the pocket on the back of her bag
and opened it. Her eyes wouldn't stop flickering around
the sentences. Out of the gathering flow of children Hugo
came running at her shouting 'I'm here!' He hurled his coat
and bag then ran back into the swirl of kids chasing each
other around the playground. Ashleigh reached down to
pick his bag up.

'Don't worry, Betsy, it's OK,' the voice near her said. Ashleigh looked round and saw that Hugo's coat had landed on
the small girl who was holding hands with the woman who
had said hi.

'Oh, sorry!' Ashleigh said, as the girl ducked and hid
behind the woman's leg.

'The after-school energy can be a bit much, specially those
older ones,' the woman said, handing Hugo's coat over. This
time Ashleigh looked at her. She was young with dramatic
eyebrows and very black hair. She didn't look like a mum.
Ashleigh wondered why she was so friendly. The woman carried on, 'Betsy's only seven, aren't you, Betsy!'

Betsy. Betsy! It must be Tara's daughter. Ashleigh looked down at the child. She was small and mousy, she didn't look up.

'OK, well, nice to meet you – bye!'

'Bye,' Ashleigh said, and watched them leave. So this was the nanny that Tara had mentioned. She watched, and as they walked away she saw the little girl's jacket, tied round her waist, slip off and fall to the ground. No one else noticed. Hugo was still running round in circles. The woman walked on, sheltering the girl from the other children surging around. Ashleigh darted forward and picked the jacket up. Ha! she thought to herself, that nanny is being relegated by me: the new babysitter. She looked over at them with a feeling of glee.

Before they reached the gate the nanny abruptly stopped and grabbed for her phone. Ashleigh was still watching, and she saw the nanny reading its screen. Saw her sagging and rubbing her face. Ashleigh read that physical reaction like words on a page. Before she even thought about why, something took over and changed her mind. Feeling kind of robotic and not like herself she hurried over to them, holding the jacket out, and spoke.

'Hey, she dropped this.'

'Oh thanks – thank you!' the nanny looked surprised. She took the jacket and folded it in between her bags. 'That's kind. I'm Samina. Who are you?'

'I'm Ashleigh,' she said. 'Or just Ash.'

'Ash, you're a star,' Samina pulled a weary face and gestured over the little girl's head. 'Seriously glad you rescued the jacket – I'm already in trouble with her mum.'

'Oh,' Ashleigh couldn't think of what to say. She wasn't good at talking to other young people, or to nice people. It was way easier to act like someone else, in front of old people.

51

Or people she hated. A loud mum-group pushing buggies did an exaggerated Excuse me and pushed between them. Samina stepped aside with a low-key roll of her eyes. Ashleigh caught the look and began to smile. They stood there and watched as the mum-group dispersed like ducks when the bread runs out. Then Ashleigh reached down to put her book back into her bag.

'Wait, is that yours?' Samina almost pounced forwards.

'Uh, yes,' Ashleigh stopped, putting the book away and instead stroked it awkwardly with her thumb.

'I swear *An Inspector Calls* is one of my top books – I love it – is it still on the curriculum? Oh my god – the stress, that ending!'

'Oh!' Ashleigh's eyes widened.

'Have you finished it yet?' Samina didn't wait for an answer. 'We did it for GCSE and I've still got my copy and my notes – the guy who wrote it was like a proper activist, and his whole argument is something my mum always used to say: We are members of one body...'

Ashleigh opened her mouth again but then didn't speak. Samina's face was vivid, full of life.

'Which sort of links into what I'm studying now,' she went on. 'Law.' Samina smiled and looked pleased with herself. 'I'm a law student.'

Ashleigh had never had an encounter like this before, not anywhere but especially not at the school gate. Samina was beautiful and Ashleigh didn't hate her. It was confusing. Ashleigh was still trying to think of something to say when the small girl started making a whining noise.

'Saminaaaaa!' Betsy had been standing out of sight but now she was pulling on Samina's arm. 'Samina!' she moaned. Ashleigh looked down at her frowning little face.

'Ha! Sorry, I got carried away there – you know what it's like,' Samina laughed as she pulled her bags together again. She touched the child lightly on the arm. 'Come on Betsy, let's go. Bye, Ash, good to meet you!'

And they left. Samina and the interrupting child; grumpy little Betsy who now lived in her old house, that small sleeping shape in the bed. Ashleigh had forgotten all about Hugo and the other shouting kids all swirling around the playground.

8

IT'S TARA'S TURN

Twice a day, every day, people gathered outside the gates of Avenue Road Primary. Grimly marking the passage of time, again and again and again. The same early ones got the spot nearest the doors. The same loners hung back. Two dads who were microcelebrities because they showed up for their own kids. The gobby mums with crisp-eating toddlers in buggies. The posh mums rolling their eyes. The hijab mums all stuck together. The nannies and au pairs tended to hang back. Dropping off and picking up, always the same. Too short for a proper conversation, but not short enough to avoid people altogether. Tara hated it.

'Tara! Your blog was just amazing, like – beyond!'

Tara moved her sunglasses up on to her head, lowered her phone, and smiled at the wide-eyed mum who had popped up in her face.

'Thanks Charlotte!'

'No, but seriously, I mean, it just was so powerful! God we just have to end this thing, this genital mutation—'

'Mutilation.'

'Mutilation I mean, so shocking.'

'Yes,' Tara agreed. They smiled for a little bit too long.

'Oh, is Mimi free for a playdate after school tomorrow?' Tara asked. 'I've got Ashleigh collecting Betsy, so she could take them both up to the park?'

Charlotte smiled even wider. 'Oh, sorry – she can't.' Her eyes were slightly alarmed. 'She's got… swimming.'

They both laughed as if in disbelief at how busy their six-year old daughters were. Tara felt a spike of shame – Betsy hadn't been on a playdate in ages. The gates were still not opening – what was going on, why was it so slow? Another mum came up and greeted Charlotte; two more were hovering nearby. They hadn't yet caught Tara's eye, but already she felt trapped. It was too late to put her sunglasses back on and retreat into her phone. She might as well give in.

'Hi Stacey,' she said, putting her phone away. Stacey was never seen without bronzer and a blow-dry. She gave Charlotte a brief diluted smile, angled herself to face Tara and announced 'Hey! So we need to catch up on book club!'

It was like feeding pigeons – as soon as Tara greeted one then a load more swooped in. Charlotte started talking to that Asian mum and Stacey looked sideways as a northern mum nearby randomly spoke to them:

'Hiya, I'm Holly!'

They paused in a circle and looked quizzically at her.

'I'm Stanley's mum,' she went on, 'I don't normally do home-time – he probably won't recognise me!' Tara and Stacey exchanged a glance. She went on, 'Book club sounds amazing, though – I used to read loads; I'd love to get back into it!'

Stacey narrowed her eyes at Holly's Tommy Hilfiger bag. It looked fake.

'So are you from, like, Manchester with that accent?' she asked.

'Leeds,' Holly replied cheerfully. 'Not even close!'

But before anyone could think of a joke about northerners the gates screeched open. Tara was relieved as they began to shuffle forwards and through into the playground area.

Stacey turned to the Asian mum. 'So, Pat… Patty…?'

'It's Pratiksha. I heard you were just talking about book club…'

'Oh, I remember you now!' said Stacey. 'You came with Emily before she moved away! Tara, who's hosting next?'

'Oh, I think it's my turn… Let me have a look.' Tara got her phone out.

Pratiksha nodded, smiling. Tara hovered her finger like she was filtering the guest list for an Oscars after-party.

'So this club, is it all mums from school, or…?' Holly the northern mum leant in, directing the question towards Tara, but Tara was still looking at her phone and it was Stacey who answered.

'Oh, well, it's… book club is full – sorry!'

'Sorry!' Tara added, looking up with a shiny high-resolution smile. Seeing Holly look from one mum to the next, she briefly felt an echo of her own dinner party isolation. But really, book club couldn't take any new people on. And her accent was a bit much. So it was probably best for everyone.

Luckily at that same moment the kids started coming out and everyone's attention moved on to the doors as they opened all the way back, releasing a bouncing flood of small humans. Tara saw Holly move away and towards her boy as he ran into her arms. She sank to her knees and hugged him with her eyes shut. The other mums were still standing there waiting.

'Charming,' Stacey said to the group as they watched Holly and the small boy leave their orbit. 'Great, so let's fix that date, then. And I claim first dibs on Ashleigh for babysitting!'

9

SAMINA INVESTS

Samina closed two of her work folders and put her pens down on one side. She ran down the list – she had completed Victim Interventions and next week's readings too. She'd annotated the shared article and written up a week of notes, with different coloured highlighters – something her friends always teased her about. She'd shared an update with her revision group and rechecked their advance study plan. She was hogging the whole kitchen table, enjoying the peace and the space before her brother and dad got home.

She shut her worn copy of *Essentials of Criminal Law*, exhaling the words 'Breaking the chain of causation!' as she arranged her work into a tidy pyramid with the smallest notepad on top. She felt a glow of deep love for these swelling folders. They reminded her of the blood donation drive the students' union did last year. She had touched the slowly inflating bag and been shocked by its warmth, it felt alive. It felt like this, like she was pouring herself into these folders, they contained her. She had never worked this hard. A-levels were a picnic in comparison.

Samina stood up and stretched her shoulders, getting a pleasing pop out of her upper spine. She looked out the window. Directly opposite was another window, half covered inside by a purple sheet. A bird flew overhead. She scanned the other windows and then down to the rows of bins running between the backs of both blocks. The broken-off baby tree was still there, hanging down. The council had replaced it twice and each time someone snapped it again. Who would do such a thing? She recalled her dad's voice: 'One hand builds and the other destroys!'

That was her dad, a pearl of ancient wisdom for every possible occasion. But he was still at work and it was quiet here at the kitchen window. Samina loved it when no one else was around. She inhaled deeply, relishing this oasis in her day, a quiet pause between her morning lecture and her study group later on. And before the place was filled up with her brother's loud friends and the smell of chicken wings. Right on cue the door slammed as Mal came in.

'Not today,' he answered her quizzical look, dropping his bag down by the door. 'Boss man says I'm first shift next time though. Off out later. Where's Dad?'

'He's not back yet. I'm going out soon too.'

Samina always made light of her workload in front of him. And she'd told their dad to stop praising her: 'You are our hope!' She smiled at her brother now, flinging himself on to the sofa. He'd recently shaved himself an eyebrow slit. Their father went mad, but she couldn't help feeling proud that her skinny little brother was now so imposing. Even if his big limbs and voice made their flat feel even smaller. He stretched his feet out in their enormous Air Jordans, and shot her his best devilish smile, with the furrowed brow.

'Shut up!' she laughed.

'Off out to your posh family job innit?'

'Don't say innit. And no I'm not. They're all right, you know!' She paused, 'Mostly. Supposed to be asking for fewer hours, but I think she's annoyed, so…'

Samina's hours kept shifting around and this getting was harder to balance with her studies. The agreement with Tara was fifteen hours a week to make up her monthly salary of £480. This was supposed to be two school days and one weekend day, but it was increasingly unpredictable. Last month they went away at Easter, and the following week Tara asked her to do double, 'to make up the hours.'

Samina sighed. She should be going soon. 'Want some help with your CV before I head off?' she asked. Unpredictable hours were her brother's reality too, at Milwards Sports. Sometimes it was a twelve-hour shift, and sometimes nothing. The WhatsApp group dropped last-minute shifts late at night with threatening comments about being 'less available'.

'Nah I'm good,' Mal kept scrolling on his phone.

When she heard about the timing of toilet breaks Samina said it was illegal, but he got angry and told her to stop showing off. It's flexible working – the gig economy! Mal described it almost admiringly, and she had held herself back. It was too soon for another fight. She felt a tender pain recalling the fireworks when he quit college. Their dad screaming what would their mother have said. He was still her little brother, even with his newly gigantic feet and limbs. We have to pick our battles, Dad, she'd said. For now.

'Did you see?' He looked up from his phone. 'There's been another car bomb. I hope Dad hasn't seen.'

'Oh god no. How many?'

'Don't know. Just seen a headline – didn't read it.'

A groan moved in Samina's throat. It was a permanently unresolved state, this sense of belonging to a place that no longer existed. They had left, and it had since become something else. What part of that are you supposed to love? Especially from the outside, and at such a distance. But on the other hand, it was precisely this shared thread – the stories from back home, the unhealing wound, yes, even the bombs – that bound their family together.

This was why she loved the law. Every case had a proper ending. Each interconnected part was necessary, like a completing a chain. Nothing dangled or straggled or was left unresolved. Not like bad stories on the news. The news just moved on and left all the mess behind. But with law, you took things that had happened and you processed them, defined them, gave them an ending. Each ending was a triumph, a deep satisfaction. And that was justice.

Justice. Her heart had thrilled to the first year opening lecture, she would never forget it. Don't come here if you're looking for answers. You have to provide the answers! The law has no answers, only the tools to examine what has already happened. You use these, and you can solve each part of the question in turn. It's on you! She laid a hand on her investments; her pyramid of files, as though gently patting a child's head.

Still, none of this helped her own family's story, their own broken chain. Of course during the war it had suddenly become cool to be Iraqi. Before that people at school didn't have any idea about what or even where Iraq was. They confused it in the worst way: 'Iran, Iraq, whatever, same difference!' She never once tired of correcting people, even when her brother gave up and said it was pointless. 'So let them think we're from Iran – it don't matter!'

Then all of a sudden people did know, and they couldn't get enough of stories about Saddam. Samina and Mal shared their family legends of gas attacks, intimidation, their own escape; and those who'd simply vanished and no one ever dared to ask. But the fashion was soon over. People got bored, the news from Iraq eventually shrank to a dutiful roundup of only the most massive bomb attacks.

At the sound of the key in the door they both turned, Mal put his phone down and said 'Hey Dad!' Their father closed the door, stepped out of his shoes and carried his bags into the kitchen area. He put them down on the side. His grey hair was neatly combed; he looked tired.

'There was another car bomb,' he said, undoing his jacket buttons.

'We know.'

'But it will be out of the news this same evening – you will see.'

'It's all about the Syrians now, Dad,' joked Mal. 'We're last year's X factor.'

Their father went back to hang his coat up by the door then he came over to the sofa and sank down next to Mal with a deep sigh.

'Come on, Dad,' Samina spoke gently. 'Don't forget the good times, the riverside trips!'

Together they tried to lure him on to his favourite conversational pasture: the sun-lit olden days. They often conspired this way. When they were little she and Mal loved his stories, again and over again. The fruit orchards. Grilled fish by the banks of the Euphrates. The trips to Lebanon. And always the poetry. Poems poems poems. 'We ate poems like you eat Cheerios!' he'd say.

Usually this worked but now they could see his mind was drawn back, worrying away and checking his phone. He went back to the kitchen area and began unloading vegetables from a cloth bag. His habit was to have a sit down and some tea first. But not today. Bomb attacks on the news were a guarantee that a how-the-mighty-have-fallen lecture was on its way. Samina breathed inwards, preparing to cut this one off in its infancy.

'How can it have come to this—'

'I know, Dad. I love you. Listen I've got to go, it's my study group.'

She could read over her notes again on the train if she got a seat. Samina scooped up her bag, put her folders carefully inside and finished off the last of her abandoned coffee. 'Ugh.' She wiped her chin and looked back at her dad who was still standing and staring at the inside of the cloth bag.

'OK, I'm off!'

He looked up.

'Take some food with you? And your nannying job?

'That's tomorrow. I hope! If she doesn't change it again!' Samina edged towards the door.

'But half of your time is wasted in getting there and back.'

'OK, Dad, I get it,' Samina didn't want to get irritated. 'Should I get some bar work instead? Nuraya says she can get me a job easy!'

She caught Mal's eye and he grinned. There was no answer to this and they both knew it. One last quick Bye and she was out the door and along the corridor to the stairs, her bag swinging as she ran.

10

TARA TRIES

'Respect, excellence and friendship, we love
Respect, excellence and friendship.
Joining hands around the world, connecting you and me, with
Respect, excellence and friendship!'

Every child in the school was packed on to and around the
stage, clutching hand-made paper flags from all over the
world. They strained their necks, hands clenched, singing
their utmost at the deep crowd of parents opposite. The
audience was perched on rows of benches, babies on laps
and phones held up high. People tutted at other people's
screens blocking their screens. The Olympics song, led by
an arm-waving music teacher balanced on a chair behind
the parents, faltered as Ms O'Keefe the headteacher picked
her way between the legs of the reception class to get to the
front.

'Good morning, parents and carers, and thank you all for
coming to Avenue Road Primary school's Olympic Pride
assembly.'

She spread her arms open and looked from side to side
at the audience of eager faces. Her hair was wrapped
round with a green scarf, and the potentially racy effect of

her purple lipstick was balanced out by the severe, black-framed glasses.

'Thanks to Ms Khalil for that charismatic musical direction! And thank you, children – you gave it your all, just like our Olympic and Paralympic heroes.'

She beamed down at them. Tara looked sideways at Giles and saw his mouth twitch slightly. Several phones went off.

'Like many of us I'm an adoptive Londoner,' she went on. 'This is the greatest city on earth – we're lucky to live here! The Olympics is coming and the whole world will be looking to us. It's a sign of London's confidence that we can celebrate our diversity. Just like your song – Respect, Excellence and Friendship.'

Two babies fussing in the audience were drowned out by a wailing sound from the middle ranks, 'Miss! Benny's weed herself again!' and a wave of giggles, faces turning with excitement. Ms O'Keefe paused majestically as a member of staff waded in and extracted a dripping child. She permitted a small smile then directed her gaze directly at the parents. She hesitated, with her eyes narrowed and her head tipped slightly, to indicate that a deep truth was on its way.

'As the Olympic torch travels we reflect on what that symbol means – the values of the Olympic Games. Our mayor says London is the most generous-hearted city on earth, and we all have our part to play in this. Generosity doesn't happen by accident. Diversity doesn't happen by accident. And communities don't happen by accident. We make these things happen. Together, we have more power than we know.'

Tara heard his derisory exhalation but didn't glance at Giles. She was straining to catch sight of Betsy who was stuck behind a taller girl in the second row.

'Our quote for the day: "Cultivation of mind teaches young people how to begin to think, how to mix with a number of equals, till they become enlightened citizens. For only by the jostlings of equality can we form a just opinion of ourselves." Now Years Five and Six are going to give one more rendition of our Olympics song, parents and carers please remain where you are and don't block the way while nursery and reception leave, followed by lower school.'

Row by row the children stood up to leave the school hall, their chattering sounds grew, the teachers shushed, and the parents tried to get photos of their kids even as they filed out of the school hall.

'More power than we know, oh bless her M&S sandals,' laughed Tara as they stood up and made their way out of the hall and into the playground. Giles was looking at his phone. She carried on, 'Didn't Betsy do well. Shame we could hardly see her for that bloody tall girl. Oh shit!' She tried to dip behind Giles as a woman came jogging towards her.

'There you are! Did you get my messages? About the next blog?'

Tara didn't break her step – she carried on and replied over her shoulder as they continued towards the gate: 'Oh, they said you were sending me a draft. I've been waiting for you!'

She and Giles headed out on to the street and he made a 'what?' noise.

'She's from No Cuts, you know,' Tara scowled. 'The FGM campaign. I did that blog but now they want more.'

'Hm, nightmare colleagues – don't get me started. I've still got that new editor trying to undermine me, driving me nuts.'

'What?'

'That woman, Faiza, whatever.' They crossed the road away from the other parents leaving the school gate. 'And if that wasn't bad enough I come to Betsy's school and get the same lecture. It's all I hear about.'

Tara couldn't be bothered to join in.

'All this Olympics and diversity hoo-haa, it makes us look like we don't know who we are. But we know exactly who we are. Olympic pride, my arse.'

Tara made some vague agreeing noises but didn't comment. She was still fuming. She would tell the FGM group that annoying woman was actually putting other volunteers off. That would shut her up. Also Giles hadn't noticed that he had just hijacked her grumble and made it into his own. He expanded on the subject for the rest of the walk home while Tara felt like her side of the conversation could have been maintained by a face drawn on to a paper bag.

They got home and pushed open the door – it was time for their coffee together before Giles went into the office. Today she hoped to tell him about her screenplay. It never felt like the right time. He checked the water tank of the Gaggia Classic espresso machine, vigorously released a jet of steam and scooped in the pre-ground.

'Where's the bloody remote for this thing?' He poked the radio/CD player on the side – the new cleaner had left it on London's Heart 106.2 and now they couldn't get back to Radio 4.

'Still can't find it,' Tara said, going to the fridge and bringing out a jar. 'I've looked everywhere.'

'So my next column might be a "new dad" thing based around the paddling pool – remember when Betsy did a crap the size of a small otter – wait, what's that?'

'It's kombucha – I told you—'

'What?!'

She put the kombucha back and sat down at the table. 'So my blog has done really well – everyone was talking about it at school the other day.'

'Mm-hm.'

'I've been developing the screenplay idea too. People need to know more about this!'

'They certainly do. Listen, you didn't find those dollars anywhere, did you?'

'From the US trip? No. Am I supposed to know where all your things are?'

'I wasn't saying that—'

'Babes, we do need to talk about childcare, though,' Tara pressed. 'Do you think Samina's OK? I've been thinking maybe Ashleigh's our best option for now. I'm not sure – can we justify having a nanny as well as the cleaner? Ashleigh is so much easier. And cheaper!'

Giles gave Tara a deadpan look. 'Another one bites the dust?' He brought over two steaming coffees and sat down opposite her. 'The fact is, if we get a new person they'll annoy you too – do you really want to go back to a stream of young Agis?'

Tara twisted a strand of hair behind her ear. Agi was their collective term for the series of au pair girls that came before Samina. That had not gone well.

'You're feisty and that's why I love you, but babes, you need to stop looking for things to get annoyed about – just because you're bored!' Giles laughed a big laugh that seemed to bounce off the walls, and ruffled his own hair into peak dishevelment.

'I'm not bored.'

Tara went to the sink and moved a few cups around. The gold-rim ones were hand-wash only. She squeezed out the sponge. She couldn't take another barrage of his relentless cocky certainty about every bloody thing in the universe. How could anyone be so sure of himself? In the past she'd felt reassured by his unassailable grip on the truth. Now she could hardly stand it. She stared out into the garden for a moment and visualised her Mindfulness pebble.

Also… There was a compliment in here. He rarely told her that he loved her. Tara couldn't remember the last time and it gave her a pinching feeling behind her eyes. She would try to accept the nice part and ignore the rest. She ran the sponge round the marble edges of the sink and removed a used tea-bag from the plug. But there was still an itch to scratch; there was just something uncomfortable about Samina. She came back to the table and sat down.

'I'm not bored,' she repeated, smiling like a reasonable person. 'But I think maybe we should just have Ashleigh for now, until I get back to work. And before you ask – yes I've been working on my screenplay, it's going really well actually.'

'Whatever.' He drained his coffee. 'Ashleigh's fine. She's a bit young, though. But summer's coming up, and if Samina goes at least we won't have to pay her holidays.'

'It's not just the money.' Tara had to scratch the itch. 'We give these people our trust, our house keys, everything! And it's not just your dollars from the trip – I'm missing a few things too – some make-up, I think.' She paused and tried to catch his eye. 'Once that trust's gone, I don't know – do we even know who Samina really is?'

Giles was checking his phone and had already departed the conversation. So she played her ace.

'Also… Samina asked me if we're getting Betsy tested for autism.'

'What!' His phone hand was frozen mid-air.

'After that time at the library.' Tara enjoyed the effect of this conversational cattle-prod. 'She must've gone off and researched it and now she's dead set on diagnosing her.'

Giles pushed the chair back and got to his feet abruptly: 'But there's nothing wrong with her.'

'Exactly. And if you get tested doesn't it stay on your records and affect school applications? We need to start looking for tutors. Anyway, it's none of her business.'

'OK, do whatever you think. Listen I've got to go. But while we're on the subject,' he looked down at her, 'you do need to keep applying for real jobs. I think you'd be less…'

'What?'

'Less… angry all the time.'

'What?'

'Well, that campaign stuff annoys you – you said so yourself. And apparently you're "not ready" for another baby. So if you want to sack the nanny then fine. But I think what you need is a job.'

He shrugged in a don't-shoot-the-messenger way, picked up his bag and headed for the door. His diagnosis went directly to her stomach; she felt the exact weight of his words as they landed there. Tara knew she would simmer over this all day and not escape from it. He could leave any time, come and go, be someplace where he mattered, somewhere he was valued and respected. He would forget this as soon as he walked out the door. It was normal for him. How comfortable that made him, how secure. How much Tara wanted to punch him in the face.

11

SAMINA TRIES

It was one of those golden London evenings. People were leaning on walls, eating out of polystyrene trays. Some boys smoked around a car vibrating with loud music. Kids and dogs tumbled in between. The hardware shop lady was reorganising her rainbow display of plastic bins and bowls in multiple sizes. The sun was still streaming through and the street smelt of fried chicken and marijuana. The fruit stalls were piled high and topped with garlands, each heap more colourful than the last.

Samina was walking back from the market with her dad, with bags of rice and oil, fresh vegetables and chicken. Her dad loved to hear every detail about university. He loved the sense of his daughter's life unfolding outwards. She could do anything, he had always told her that. And she delighted in bringing home her adventures in that world. Yesterday between lectures Samina had dropped into her university's Feminist Society, they were holding a recruitment drive.

'It's funny – you know, it was mostly about clothes. There were things called Reclaim the Night and Reclaim the Cunt. But mostly clothes. How to wear them, or not wear them, and how to prevent others from wearing things you don't like. So they like slutwalks but not Page Three. And as for the hijab—'

'You know absolutely how I hate that thing too.' He flinched as he turned to face her, his dark eyes suddenly serious. 'Promise me you will never take up the fashion for it like these other young girls.'

'But Daddy, they're always saying how oppressed we are!' She'd crash-landed them into the subject, and this wasn't the moment. She looked sideways at him and couldn't resist his determined face.

'Don't rush out making your statements into this world before you truly understand what others are capable of,' he pronounced. 'You should walk a month instead of crossing a river.' What did that even mean? Samina sighed. 'And then, your work as a nanny?' he asked.

'Tara? I don't know,' Samina sighed deeply. 'I still don't know what to do about that FGM blog of hers – she quotes me on the "horrific abuse" when all I actually said was it doesn't exist where we come from. She made it up!'

He frowned, still looking at the ground.

'And she's – she thinks she's trying to do the right thing but she's... so angry,' Samina continued. 'But she's angry with everyone, so at least it's nothing personal. You should've seen her sacking their old cleaner. Right in front of me and her husband and daughter!'

Samina tailed off, suddenly insecure. Tara's new habit of announcing last-minute schedule changes by text was getting worse. No more signing-off with a smiley. Maybe it was personal?

'It is not easy to know a person,' her dad changed the carrier bag from one hand to the other, 'and these work situations they can flow in either direction. It's been... eight months now?'

'Nine. The whole academic year. This way it's no maintenance loans until my final year, and we all know how much I love a long-term finance strategy,' she looked her dad and he smiled. 'But I tried to talk to Tara about diagnoses for autism, and she really hated that.'

'I told you not to. No one will thank you for this. What did she say?'

'That it was not my job and none of my business and never to mention it again. But Betsy's having a hard time at school, I've even seen it in the playground with my own eyes, the other kids wind her up until she lashes out,' Samina looked at the ground. 'Tara used to talk about it but now it's suddenly taboo. I thought it was my job, that I was doing the right thing.'

'Ah, always trying to fix things. Your mother would be proud,' he looked at her. 'I on the other hand would advocate a more pragmatic approach: you need the job, so keep the job!'

They walked on between the stalls and the shops, past the braid bar, the nail bar, and the barbers with the ancient poster of Will Smith. Some kids ran out of a phone shop, a boy on a bike bumped up on to the pavement and back down into the road again, Samina watched as he popped an impressively long wheely.

'Your mother, she would always say,' he looked up and away, as though he might see her in the distance, 'she would say the power that we wield over others is far greater than we know.'

'We don't live alone, we members of are one body,' Samina almost chanted, no longer sure whether she'd actually heard her mother say these words or whether they'd been implanted by repetition.

Towards the end of the block they neared a group of men standing outside the Rose & Crown, smoking and gripping pints of lager. One of them reeled away and lurched in front of them. ''Ere,' he shouted into Samina's face. She saw his eyes and wet mouth. 'All right, love.' he grinned and swayed.

Samina was used to unwanted attention, but not when she was with her father. She looked away, concentrating her gaze on a stall heaped with unnaturally shiny apples. There was a silence as they both stepped to the side and made a diversion around the man. Samina focused on the apples, she could feel the men's stares. On the other side of him they continued along the pavement without saying a word. Her neck felt prickly as they walked on. But before she could feel any relief the man shouted after them: 'Oi. Oi love.'

Despite herself Samina glanced back.

'Wanna go halves on a bastard?'

His fellow drinkers broke into throaty cackles as she turned away again. She felt her cheeks flush with anger as she and her dad walked on, side by side, in silence.

'Hm,' her father's face was deadpan. 'An equitable proposal, perhaps, but not the most eligible of suitors.'

There was a beat before they caught each other's eye and burst into gales of laughter, so strong they swayed into each other and their shopping bags collided.

12

ASHLEIGH UNDERSTANDS

Ashleigh was inside the school gate, hovering at the back of the slow crowd and giving out small polite greetings to the mums and kids and teachers who knew her. Even though she did regular pickups it still felt funny to come back, the school looked so small. Her own school, Selby High, was only ten minutes away. Lots of kids came down to pick up younger siblings. But Morgan was at football, and Ashleigh was here for work. It was for Tara — she had now been upgraded from evening babysitter to after-school pickup. She was here to collect Betsy and take her up to Bonjour Les Amis.

The teacher smiled and waved across the bustling playground as she gestured for the child to go over. Ashleigh waved as the girl walked towards her, holding her bag in her arms. She was small for her age, and according to Charlotte and Stacey's kids, she liked biting people.

'Hello,' said Ashleigh. There was no reply and Betsy didn't seem to remember that they'd met the other day, with Samina.

The child stood there holding her bag and not looking at Ashleigh's face. Finally she spoke: 'What's your name?'

'You know my name. It's Ashleigh. Remember me from last week?'

'I don't like it. It sounds... dead.'

Ashleigh nearly laughed the comment off, but something in her recognised the solemn expression. Instead of doing her cheerful self she put her head to one side thoughtfully, and replied: 'Maybe I am dead. How would you know?'

'You would smell bad.'

'But not straight away – that takes a lot longer. What's your name?'

'You know my name too. It's Betsy.'

Ashleigh frowned, as though she was considering the possibility of this name. The child was wearing a large duffle coat even though it was summer, and sensible Start-Rite shoes. She stared back at Ashleigh through her glasses.

'Betsy... I like it, but to me you look like... an Ursula.'

'No. No, that's not me.'

'It means like a bear. Bears are brilliant – bears can see in colour, unlike most mammals. And they're clever predators.'

'I saw a bear on TV, capturing an alive fish.'

Betsy spoke deliberately as she accepted Ashleigh's offer of carrying her bag. They walked slowly out of the school grounds and along the sunny pavement together. They ignored the small gangs of kids bursting past them, full of home-time energy, jumping and pushing and making monkey sounds. The kids charged ahead, howling and wind-milling their book bags round and round. They shoved each other into the bushy privet hedges shouting 'hedge-ucation!'

'Who are your friends?' Ashleigh asked.

'I don't like friends.'

'Me neither!' Ashleigh was caught off-guard by the heat of her own response. They continued in silence for a block. The girl was a lot smaller than Ashleigh's own sister, but Ash felt a warm throwback feeling as they walked along together.

A family was coming towards them, the toddler holding an ice cream that was melting down over her hand. She licked at one side and the ice cream fell off its cone on to the ground. She started crying, and the mum bent down and promised her another one in a cooing voice. The man was carrying a baby in a sling. As they walked on they talked about should they have the salmon for dinner. Both girls slowed as the family went by. There was a pause, then they looked at each other and exchanged a certain glint that wasn't yet a smile.

'Oh yes, darling, salmon for dinner, lo-o-ovely,' Ashleigh mimicked under her breath, pitch perfect, and Betsy giggled. Neither was sure exactly what, but some kind of discovery was taking place. Betsy looked up at her.

'Ashleigh, can we talk more about being dead?'

Ashleigh smiled. And as they walked on they shared descriptions of the process of bodily disintegration and decay, thought about why bones and teeth lasted the longest, compared theories on how food went mouldy, and exchanged ideas about dead pets and autumn leaves. How was dying a part of actual death, they wondered. Because if you weren't dead you had to still be alive, so how could you be a bit of both?

'My granny once died, but I didn't see it because I wasn't born,' Betsy said. 'Do you know any dead people?'

Ashleigh was now good at blocking her mother out of these moments. It happened automatically so no one knew. She paused for a moment then described in animated detail a picture of death she'd once seen on a school trip to the British Library. It was an ancient book inside a glass cabinet. The book was called *On the Fabric of the Human Body*, and the picture was of some Latin medical man. He was wearing a flowery robe – medieval people always had the worst clothes – and he was peeling open a person and spreading out their veins.

'It's the look in his eye,' Ashleigh said. 'He's almost winking at you – he's like… you might think this is gross, but it's actually amazing. I'll take you to see it one time.'

'I love veins.' Betsy raised her hands and turned them to examine the insides of her wrists. 'See, they look blue but if you bleed it's red. And when you die then I think it goes brown, and brown is the deadest colour of all.'

They listed some brown things that were dead and went on to observe that old people like teachers and parents were sort of already beginning to die, in a way, what with all their wrinkly skin and forgetfulness. They noticed that most of the Death words started with D – there was also deteriorate, decline, and decompose.

'And dump!' Betsy shouted, her voice squeaky with excitement, and Ashleigh laughed, and they became, on the short walk to Bonjour Les Amis, firm allies.

13

SAMINA TURNS

Samina came up the escalator, stepped over its grinding grey teeth, and swiped out of the Tube station barriers. A gust of stale underground air chased her into the outside world. She was buzzing, all the way there she had worked through her Dispute Resolution flashcards and not got a single one wrong. She waved at the old station guy, he was writing up a white-board sign cheering on the Team GB heroes. Outside on the street was a busker, playing guitar and singing in the sunlight.

She hovered. She was early and had some time to spare, she paused a few steps beyond the busker, listening to her song. It was an Amy Winehouse cover, dirty and beautiful, just like this city, Samina thought. Here I am right in the middle of one of the world's great cities, where you emerge from deep underground straight into live music, right here on the street, with all the people of the world bustling around me – me, here at the heart of the whole thing.

She reversed and reached into her jeans pocket for a pound. 'Cheers, darlin',' the singer called out as Samina dropped the coin into the paper cup. As she moved away she felt a thrill, a lightness, as though a magical London electricity was rising out of the pavement, up through her trainers and into her body. The people streaming by her all had their own lives, loves, and purposes. She felt the luck of her own purpose. Get ready for me, London. The energy shone out of her and she couldn't hold in a smile as she set off down the busy pavement.

Everyone was out in T-shirts, their bare skin loving the sunshine. Every seat outside every café was filled with basking bodies; faces raised, shoulders unhunched. It was the power of summer, Samina thought, bringing this city out of itself each year in a way that never stopped being miraculous. Out of the winter and out they all came, London's pasty bodies, tattoos and smiles, summoned forth and blessed by the sunshine.

Bless. Samina once had a primary school teacher who used to say 'Bless'. Ms Harris – she was old and round, not quick enough to keep up with the naughtier kids, but always kind. 'Bless.' Not bless you, or bless anything: just 'Bless'. Samina had loved this – she had copied it before her English was fluent. It felt like a London thing to say. Dad said British people weren't religious, so they mustn't go talking about their faith. But clearly Britain had some of its old ways – old habits were still there. Bless.

Further away from the station and the shops ended and the flats and houses took over. White houses with big windows, red-brick houses with stained glass in their doors, small blocks of flats, containing lives of people who enjoyed their tidy front gardens. They were blessed too, but London was its own kind of blessing for Samina. Maybe all cities have this magic, she thought, for those who really need it. Maybe you love a place more when you need it. And it gives you more because you notice it. She imagined the faded photos in the Baghdad album. The flat-coloured images had turned themselves into memories by sheer force of having been looked at a thousand times. But this city looks right back at me, thought Samina. It can see me, see who I am. A place is only real if it can see you. This is my home, and this is why I'm me.

This wasn't the plan. She had made a promise to herself when they first arrived, to love their lost mother and to hold on to their lost land, for ever. It was a question of loyalty, a test of love. She could see it in her dad, in the way he would never belong here, not like she and Mal did. She didn't talk about feeling like a Londoner with her dad, though, she didn't want to hurt his feelings. Their family had subtly divided in this way, not just their accents; more than that, deeper down.

Samina had got her grades back before the holidays and had, again, got the highest marks in her year.

'Can't you be in the papers again?' her dad asked. He treasured that newspaper article with the smiling photo showing her and the three others who'd got straight As.

She laughed, 'That was school, Dad! There will be no articles, just exams and then more exams.' And then more. She'd forgotten how to read for pleasure, she was always processing. It was so intensive she worried all her first-year work was buried beneath the new content that was endlessly filed into her brain.

She felt like a factory that never stopped. It was about keeping everything going on at the same time, the job and the studying. Even now in the holidays. While she was at work her friend Zahrah was doing notes on a court visit, and she'd do the next one in return. The tutors had no mercy if you hadn't done the reading preparation, you'd be shown up immediately. Onwards and onwards.

Mal asked her what kind of sports car she'd buy him when she made partner in some big law firm. That'll be a second-hand bike for you, baby boy! She laughed to herself and turned off the main street. She walked down past her favourite tree, the one with a twisty trunk bursting through the wall. She paused to smell a small white rose leaning on a railing. Dad insisted Baghdad was full of roses but she couldn't imagine it. To her they were the most British flower – not over the top, just quietly confident. She turned the next corner into Tara's street.

This was the moment of turning from her student self into her work self. She dug around in her bag for the key. Sometimes she would try to guess, key in the door, whether she was going to meet big-smile Tara, or thundercloud Tara. This was the truth of being inside a family, but not part of the family. She pushed the door open. She decided that if Tara smiled, she would definitely tell her about the exams that were coming up, and ask whether it might be OK to do fewer hours. Just ask her, straight out.

How hard could it be?

14

TARA ATTACKS

Tara heard the door and she knew it was definitely time. She was sitting at the table. There was just no point being a wimp about these things – they simply couldn't have a person they didn't trust. Plus Giles had told her she needed a proper job, and this would show she hadn't lost her edge. She took down and redid her ponytail, then quickly went and sat on the sofa instead. She heard Samina in the hall, humming gently and taking off her shoes and jacket. She walked into the room with a smile, still holding her bag.

'Hi there. Lovely day outside – it's so sunny!'

Usually they'd sit down together and get their diaries out, run through Betsy's activities and get the week's hours arranged in advance. Tara took a deep breath. Giles had definitely agreed this was the best way. She was sitting with her back straight. She launched straight in.

'Samina, we need to talk. Several items have recently gone missing – it's causing a lot of concern, and so we're going to have to let you go.'

Samina stared blankly at her. Her hands were still holding the bag. Tara stared back but the stare didn't change, it went on for ages, so to fill the space Tara continued: 'Samina, do you understand?'

'Let me go? Are you firing me? What are you talking about?'

'Let's not pretend, Samina. It's not just one thing, it's a number of things. We can't find the remote for the Bose and I've looked everywhere.' Tara gestured, her hands suggesting a large empty space. 'And some dollars from Giles' work trip – I've looked all over. It's a matter of trust, and I – well, we – we don't think we can work together any more, Samina.'

Tara kept on pronouncing the name. Samina kept on staring back at her. She gulped and blinked twice. A flashcard popped randomly back into her mind: Indictable Offence. Her eyes stared right into Tara's eyes, around her face and back to her eyes again as though looking for evidence.

'I hope you can understand,' Tara added more slowly, trying to sound calm.

'No. I don't.' She dropped her bag on the floor.

'OK, well, look, we're prepared to pay you to the end of the month—' Tara said in a reasonable voice.

'But it's not true. That is what I'm telling you!'

Tara felt a rising panic, thinking, Shit, I shouldn't have done it like this. We should have said we couldn't afford her. This was a mess. She inhaled deeply.

'Samina, the decision is made. As I said, we'll pay you to the end of the month, and that's actually over a week of money for nothing. And I'm happy to give you a reference as long as—'

'You're accusing me of stealing but you would give me a reference?'

'Don't shout at me, Samina! Basically you're lucky we're not involving the police.'

'I'm not lucky!' Samina didn't blink. 'Call the police. Because I am innocent. And I am not the one who invents quotes in my blog!'

'Really, Samina?' Tara's eyes narrowed. 'That's how you want to do this?' She was perched on the sofa with her ankles together, her neck muscles frozen. How dare she accuse me like that! Tara's blood rose. She was judging me the whole time! She made her voice deeper.

'A police warning would go on your records, Samina – is that what you want?'

Samina made a noise in her throat as she picked her bag up off the floor and left the room. Tara heard her speaking in Arabic as she grabbed her shoes and coat and slammed the front door. What the hell was that, thought Tara – some kind of spooky Islamic curse? Shit, shit. What if she tries to get revenge, or report us somehow? *Shit.* Bringing up the blog, though – what the hell? She had meant to change the names. Too late now. She stood up and paced around, winding her hair up into twists and biting the skin inside the corners of her mouth. She was sweating. She called Giles. His phone went straight to voicemail.

'It's me. Call me. That went disastrously. Call me!'

She crossed the room and peered out of the front window. She could still see Samina walking away on the street outside, almost out of sight. Tara rang Giles again, and again, straight to voicemail. One more time – oh for god's sake, why could she never get through to him when it really mattered?

Tara paced around the kitchen and stopped in the middle. She held up her phone again and scrolled down the contacts. She could feel her pulse. Is decent childcare too much to bloody ask? And she was so confrontational about it – so aggressive! There was no point waiting for the worst to happen. Her hands were shaking but she could fix this. Attack was the best form of defence. It rang.

'Yes, hello? Yes my name is Tara Birling, and I'd like to report a case of theft and also harassment, please, and I know who it was and I'm going to want to press charges.'

15

HOLLY MOVES UP

The Children's Social Care Unit was small compared to the other council departments, but there it was, right in the middle, in an office in a block on a concrete space at the junction of two hectic London roads. There were plants and cups everywhere, desk fans, mug trees, fruit teas, a pin board and a white board. Heaps of folders, ring binders and boxes lay about, wall charts and calendars filled every space. Stationery corner. Genius paper clip holders. A picture of a kitten hanging by its claws saying Is It Friday Yet?

Holly remembered her first day here. Barbara the manager had shown her to the worst desk in the room. She had sat in the chair with worn-out arm rests and looked around fully expecting to see a sign saying You don't have to be crazy to work here but it helps. And there on a nearby shelf was the next best thing: a dancing plastic flower with sunglasses on. She wondered how long she'd last. Temping didn't pay well but at least you were free to leave.

But here she was over two years later, right at the heart of things, with a window desk, and her own personal mug in the team collection of mugs with jokes about wine and gin and sex. The most earnest team member had pointed out that this was inappropriate considering most of their clients' circumstances. He was the odd one out though. Or the not-odd one in, in among the motley bunch of social workers that had become Holly's work family.

They all came from different backgrounds, and it was the first London job where no one had teased her about her accent. That was refreshing. And the daily work was so intense, so filled with unspeakable darkness and common goodness, that Holly felt she'd fallen in with a local version of the X-Men. Finally it was somewhere she wanted to stay. Somewhere that was worth Stanley being in after-school club, or round at her downstairs neighbour Maureen's. She'd started out as an admin temp, now she was the team clerk, and already she had her eye on the next rung.

Lucky she was a fast learner because the vacancy rates had gone mad. She was in the duty team doing immediate and short-term calls on child safety cases. They were seven people doing a ten-person team workload. They could barely keep up, but it meant she learnt more. It was the first place she'd had the feeling of a straight line. Not just putting things in the right places, like her student job at the coleslaw factory, the never-ending rows of pots on a conveyor belt. This straight line was the effect of their decisions on other people. It was like a flood defence, or a beam keeping the roof from caving in. They were holding back disasters.

Holly had seen at least half the team in tears. Everyone hates social workers, they all knew that, but the verbal abuse from client families still took its toll. For some reason it was always worse on a Friday. Or at full moon. Or national holidays. But maybe they said this to cheer themselves up. Some of them didn't need any cheering up though. Like Maria. Maria had immaculate hair and upper arms like Michelle Obama. She was a natural boss. She was also feared and hated among the clients for her track record at removals.

CHAPTER 15

Even some of the team said she went too far, but no one said it to her face.

The fact that the rest of the world had crazily strong views about their work brought them closer, and was the source of most of their office humour. 'Even the traffic wardens cross the road when they see me coming.' 'Nice gladiator sandals – reckon you'll need them today.' It was one way of coping with it. 'Never a dull moment.' News of the government's promise of a £10 billion cut in welfare was greeted in the office with farmyard animal sound effects. The police had installed a panic button in Maria's home after the last death threats.

Holly always took any opportunity to work with Maria. Sometimes she got to go along with her when young clients needed an escort between carers. They'd done a couple of long car journeys together with kids who couldn't sit still and had to go to the toilet every half hour. One time they sat for hours in family court waiting with a girl who had to appear just for one minute so she could be asked if she knew why she was being adopted. The girl sat in silence, deep in the pages of *Bliss* magazine. Holly took the chance to ask Maria what she liked about the job.

'What I like is, you're getting paid to think, to use your judgement.' Maria was in a generous mood. 'And that's powerful. But it's completely thankless. You already know everyone hates us for it. But what we do is we stop the worst from happening. That's our job.'

'And how do you know when you've done that?' Holly asked. The girl looked up at them with a brief mocking smile then back to her magazine.

'You don't. Although,' she allowed a dry laugh, 'Last week Barbara got a hug in the street off someone who threw

87

scalding tea at her from an upstairs window five years ago. But normally you only get the tea, not the hug. In the short term, you only know for certain about outcomes when they go wrong,' Maria dropped her voice. 'And when that happens it's always, always our fault. You better learn to handle that.'

Holly often bumped into clients, some at school, others on the street. She had the same cheery way with everyone, no matter what she knew about them. Maybe that was her X-men superpower, being able to say hello to someone who battered their kids. The team was mostly out and about on community visits in the afternoons, and this was when she did all her admin calls, filing and bookings. It was flexible up to a point, she had made it to Stan's first school assembly thanks to Barbara. And if she felt guilty about her boy being in after-school club, at least it meant she didn't have to face those hate-smiling school-gate mums with their stupid book club. She and Stan were fine with her old neighbour Maureen's help.

Only today she'd called Maureen to get Stan from after-school club. They were sat watching *Neighbours* and eating York Fruits Jellies when she got there. 'You're a life-saver Maureen.' She hugged her as she came in the door, then bent down to hug her boy. Maureen didn't like social workers though, they were snobs, she said, the lot of them – all they did was judge people on how nice their house was, and if the house was messy take their kids off them.

'What if we went round and looked in their houses?' she said. 'And anyway – do they think bad things don't happen in nice houses?'

Holly didn't know what to say to that.

16

LUDI IS LATE

Morgan's football practice was about to end and Ludi was down the Holloway Road on his way back from a job. He would only be a bit late if he put his foot down. It was the full on evening rush and he was in the van singing along to Capital FM at the traffic lights.

'Call me maybe!' He did the phone-hand gesture, him and Morgan had sung it all the way to school this morning. Half-way through he caught the eye of someone in the next car. A woman was smiling up at him. He turned away, jabbed the radio over to Five Live, drummed the steering wheel and looked up at the still-red traffic lights.

The woman on the radio was on about the Olympic torch. Ludi slightly moved his head to be able to glance back at the smiling face, but she was looking straight ahead. Ages ago Ashleigh used to tease him, asking if he fancied her teacher. She'd say he wasn't allowed to get a girlfriend; 'We don't want a new mum – we've got you!' And he would quickly change the subject. He still couldn't bear it, that was the truth.

Diane. The word still hurt his insides, like he'd swallowed something sharp. The mother of his girls, the love of his life. Yes, still. And it hurt even more to remember happy times, them being all right. Here's what you could have won! The lights were green. Ludi changed gear and revved. He knocked the radio off and drove grimly.

Remembering her always moved in the same direction, he always got the sliding feeling. Small things, it was, with Diane. Like the mugs. There were special mugs that no one else could use because they had a message. Ashleigh was only a baby. She was tiny back then. That time Diane's mate Sian came round and he made them tea.

'Milk and sugar?'

'Just the tip of the spoon,' Sian said. He remembered it was funny – that tough Jamaican girl asking all dainty. And he made a joke of getting a really tiny bit of sugar on the spoon and they laughed. But the second her friend left Diane had a fit because he'd used the teddy-bear mug.

'Anyone can see what you're doing!' She smashed it to pieces in the sink. 'Look what you made me do!'

Ludi knew it wasn't good to go over this stuff. He rubbed his face. Some memories stick like something in your eye and you can't see past it. That's how bad memories stay. That's what it got like back then. She'd lost another pregnancy. He'd go down the pub after work, couldn't stand being in the flat. She was always up at Scabby Mark's getting gear – he hated coming home.

The traffic was moving slowly now in a long line ahead of him. Buses that he couldn't see round the edge of, and cyclists weaving in between. It moved then stopped again at the next lights. He sat there. You never knew with Diane. One night she'd be going on about she loved him, she'd be nothing without him, couldn't live without him. Then just like that she'd turn back into an alky talking shit then snoring like a chainsaw. Mouth open. And the next morning, same old. This very same van, he was in, when he finally realised. Realised how wrong it was.

CHAPTER 16

Ludi looked down to check his phone on the seat next to him. He was going to be five minutes late, ten max. He gripped the steering wheel hard and could see the bones of his hands.

It was a long time ago, when he realised. What took him so long. Stupid. He was on his way with Steve going to Green Lanes but he'd left his drain rods out his bag, so they had to drop back home to collect them. And he asked Steve up for a tea, big mistake. Within two minutes it was 'What you give him that one for?' Diane had swept the mug off the side, tea everywhere, cup smashed against the tiles. She did it so hard her T-shirt pulled up high, out of breath she was that mad, screaming, 'Now look what you've done.' It was his birthday mug, Best Dad Ever. Shattered into bits and splinters.

She'd never done it in front of other people before. They backed out the door, him and Steve, with all that crazy shit smashing and bouncing off walls around them. Straight back down, outside and into the van. The relief of moving away, of traffic news on the radio. They had both sat there, eyes fixed on the brake lights of the van in front. After a few minutes feeling his own heart beating and wishing he was dead, he heard Steve go, 'Fuck's sake, Ludi, what's up with her?'

And that was when he knew.

Ludi snapped himself out of it, checked his mirrors, changed gear and the traffic moved off again. It was too much digging around, it brought him down. The van was his own safe world and he didn't want it full of that memory. He pulled up round the corner, turned off the engine, pulled the handbrake. He jumped out with his hands tightly bunched, slammed the door and locked it. He made it to the school gate only four minutes late.

17

ASHLEIGH READS

Ashleigh had been upgraded again. Within a fortnight she had gone from babysitting when Betsy was already asleep, to after-school pickups, and now she could be entrusted with the entirety of the sacred Bedtime Routine. The way parents talked about it you'd think it was open-heart surgery. Ashleigh knew what she was doing, she had done it all those years with Morgan. But she always paid close attention to parental instructions, just in case. Kids didn't mean to snitch but it could easily happen.

When Tara finally stopped giving instructions and left the house Ashleigh rolled her eyes conspiratorially at Betsy. At last! They were sitting on the floor near Betsy's bookshelf next to a gigantic stuffed tiger and an antique child's chair. Betsy's hair was tufted up at the back. Her pyjamas were emblazoned with smiling cupcakes and the words Daddy's Little Princess, in contrast to her fixed, dark stare. She rolled and fiddled with the hem of her pyjama sleeve. She looked to Ashleigh like a cartoon girl, with her big head and tiny hands and feet.

'OK – boring stuff first then good stuff after,' Ashleigh said, 'or as I like to call it: deferred gratification.'

'Grat-ifi-cation,' Betsy echoed.

They hurried to the bathroom so Betsy could brush her teeth and pee, then they constructed a duvet nest beside her bed and took turns to choose books. Here was one of Ashleigh's favourites, *What Do People Do all Day?* She'd say, 'Look, everyone has their job to do, and how many different jobs there are in the world, and what do your daddy and mummy do for a job?' Most kids had no idea what their own parents did. Betsy was one of them. She stared away from the open pages, grinding her teeth, twizzling her hair, then muttered that she didn't know.

'That's not like you, Betsy. You're a girl who likes to know things.'

'Yes, I am.' Betsy looked up, pleased.

Ashleigh smiled. Maybe this girl could be different from her parents. It was possible after all. She knew it was unfair to harvest information about the parents from their children. It was second-hand, unscientific and completely beneath her. But it was also irresistible. To hear that Mummy shaved her front-bum hair, or that Daddy cried in the shed, these sour little glimpses showed the adults in a pitiful light. Ashleigh loved them. Eventually she moved on to her knees and gathered their books into a pile.

'OK, let's get you into bed,' she said, 'and we can read some more.'

'No, wait – first we have to make everyone right.' Betsy stood up and began to arrange her toys. Baby Annabel was leaning on a stiff china doll wearing a velvet dress. There was a Lalaloopsie Sweetie Candy Ribbon doll with her own house, and three Furbies.

'Mummy took their batteries out and she said a bad word,' Betsy confided.

Then a green turtle and a hedgehog, and a row of plastic Moshi Monsters. Betsy demonstrated how they all had to be looking at each other so they didn't stare at her in the night.

Also her slippers should be pointing away at the top end of the bed, and the bottom end of the duvet cover had to be tucked under the mattress so that her feet were protected and nothing could get in. Ashleigh showed that she understood these to be practical and necessary measures.

'What about him?' she gestured to the stuffed tiger on the floor by the chair.

'No she watches them. Don't move her.'

Betsy clambered into her bed dragging *A Golden Treasury of Nursery Classics* with her. She turned straight to 'Goldie Locks and the Three Bears' and pushed the open book towards Ashleigh, who was sitting on the floor beside her. Two pages in Ashleigh slipped into reading in a flat voice, and gave the bears stupid voices. Especially Baby Bear. She couldn't help herself. He was such a snake, always crying like that.

The girl blinked. 'But Baby Bear is cute.'

'Baby bears don't stay cute for long.' Ashleigh's voice was weary. Obviously Mummy and Daddy were going to buy him a brand-new bed. She got through all the porridge, chairs and beds and to the end. Betsy didn't say anything, she pulled her duvet to her chin and looked up at Ashleigh. She was so small.

'OK, then.' Ashleigh looked at her and softened. 'How about one more?' The mood was restored with a much more satisfactory story about a magpie who tricks all the villagers. Everything was cosy, Ashleigh got to her feet and whispered good night. She moved to the door.

'Ashleigh!' Betsy lifted her head off the pillow.

'Yes?'

'When will you come again?'

'Soon, I hope.' Ashleigh spoke quietly from the open door. 'Now off you go to sleep!'

'I hope too.' She raised herself up on one elbow. 'Ashleigh!'

'Yes?'

'Before you go can you put my music on and can you move the light so there's no shadows?'

'Of course.' Ashleigh moved gently round the room setting everything just right, with Betsy watching her. It made her feel a bit like an angel. 'There, like this. All ready for a good night's sleep!'

The girl curled back into her bedding with a small sigh. 'Good night, Ashleigh!'

'Good night,' she said, and softly pulled the door shut behind her.

Back outside on the landing Ashleigh closed her eyes and stood completely still. She could feel her own skin. She waited, then opened her eyes and moved downstairs. Her steps were soft and soundless on the thick stair carpet. She breathed out slowly, relishing each footfall, her hand sliding down the silky banister. The energy was coming back, the thrill began to flood through her and into her blood. This was her space, her joy, her triumph. *Goldie Locks?* Forget it. This was how to do it. With her skills, her craft. This was for no one but herself.

At school everyone had online lives, she watched this carefully. She knew about a philosopher called Plato who described prisoners looking at shadows on the back of a cave. They were like this – they weren't seeing the real thing. Sometimes she joined in, just doing the bare minimum. There were group chats like #famshame and #famfail where they shared stuff from their homes. They secretly recorded their mums screaming at them. One filmed her dad taking a shit. Ashleigh had added a couple of her sister, falling over, spilling food. But it wasn't real.

This was real, and it was hers. She touched the curled end of the banister and stood in the hall, pretending it was hers, acting like it was all hers. She was the only person who knew that nothing else mattered apart from this exact moment. Ashleigh felt like she could become a famous philosopher. Or an artist. She could construct a Now. Her whole life was inside a moment, only now was real. She was still working on this thought and it got better every time. She struck a pose in the middle of the kitchen.

'You know my method,' she quoted out loud. 'It has long been an axiom of mine that the little things are infinitely the most important.'

Unlike most Sherlock fans Ashleigh knew the books as well as the show. She sucked her cheekbones in at the reflective surface of the microwave. 'I'm She-lock. And who needs dead bodies when you can investigate live ones?' She occupied the space with all her senses, breathing it in, walking around like it was her own life. She was trying it on, and it felt good. Why shouldn't she? It felt right.

Her own home felt wrong. Their flat was cramped, stepping on Lego when she came down her ladder, Morgan always trying to poke through her stuff, Dad doing a thundering piss with the door half open. But here she was alone and in charge. Here she was at home. It felt so necessary.

'This unfortunate juvenile endures life with two adults of limited originality, despite their unusually abundant resources,' Ashleigh swept her hands to direct the audience's gaze toward the rocking horse in the front window. Mimicking a journalist talking to the camera she walked through into the adjoining room, paused, and gestured: 'The Samsung 46-inch LCD television with edge lighting is how the male pacifies the females of his pack, who might otherwise challenge his dominant position.'

She turned to the bookshelves, floor to ceiling. Many more than in any other house she'd ever been in. She ran a finger along them, turning her head from side to side to read the titles. Why didn't titles all go in the same direction? Did upwards titles mean a happy ending, while titles leading down the spine could only end in despair? Most went down. She trailed her fingers onwards. *Sapiens*, *Room*, *The Sense of an Ending*, *A Golden Age*, *State of Wonder*.

Was there an equivalent of the cheap vodka, the Froot Loops? But wait. Here. She zoomed in on a colourful shelf filled with unhappiness. It was self-help central, Ashleigh pulled one out and read aloud to her imaginary audience: *Quiet: The Power of Introverts in a World that Can't Stop Talking*. Yes, she added aside, Tara's problem is that she just can't get heard. She gave a hollow laugh and moved on to *The Geeks Shall Inherit the Earth: Popularity, Quirk Theory and Why Outsiders Thrive After High School*. Why did self-help books have such stupid long titles? She pulled out another one. *What Children Need to Be Happy, Confident and Successful*.

They're trying to get her to take over the world? Ashleigh's eyes narrowed. They want Betsy to be Sasha Fierce? These people, they parent so hard it's not even funny. Success at any cost. She'd often heard parents say it, 'We just want the best for them.' She heard that and thought, go on – finish the sentence: the best for them at any price. No matter what. Not a minute wasted, not a pound unspent, in the mission to guarantee that their totally ordinary offspring get ahead, that they succeed. That they win. That they go and eat sushi and play tennis in a shiny school with their shiny hair.

She shoved the book back angrily. Did they really love their kids so much more? 'We just want the best for them!' Ashleigh mimicked in a whiny defensive voice. Whatever. She was never going to have kids. What a loser's game. Why didn't her dad know about books like this though? Or anything else. But it was only a shadow of a question, it didn't last. Because basically, it didn't matter. She flicked her hair back. None of that mattered. 'Because I sprang, fully formed, from the head of Zeus.' As she spoke she arched an eyebrow at her audience, then returned, grinning, to the shelves.

Good Gut Bugs, *The Healthy Gut Cookbook*, *The Secrets of Perfect Digestion*, *The Divine Gut*. Yuk. A gut shelf. Who knew! That explained the Gaviscon habit. She moved along, pulling out and replacing a few others at random, handling them tenderly. *A Room of One's Own*. She'd heard of this one before and eagerly opened it. The title gave her an electric feeling. She read a few pages at speed and found the woman to be quite boastful, but that title still stuck, as though someone had diagnosed her. All the many things that a book could do, she mused.

Moving on, a light purple spine featuring a bitten apple: *EROTICA*. She flipped its pages with gathering disappointment. There were country girls being whipped by lords with flaring nostrils, and fleet-footed nymphs being ravished by swans and goats. Nothing like what the boys at school shared on their phones, but at least a change from the *Fifty Shades* littering all her other homes.

She dragged a chair round to climb up and reach to the top. A row of old classics, but not just for show, she noted respectfully – they were well-worn with cracked spines. Perhaps they were old school textbooks? Yes, some of them had notes in the margins. *Hamlet*. It had Giles Birling written inside the cover. She checked to see if his annotation was any good.

'Hamlet – prevaricating.' Then it was crossed out and the word Procrastinating written above. Ashleigh rolled her eyes. He'd be lucky to get a C+.

Some were dotted with brown stains like tea, the colour leached into the pages inside. They smelt like oldness. Near the end was a slim poetry volume with a rough cloth cover. She stood on the chair, reading out loud using her school voice. Then another one in her work voice: nicer, posher. Wait. As she moved the book from one hand to the other something slipped out from between the pages and fell to the floor. She held the page with her finger. Aha. The first line was underlined with black ink: 'Woman much missed how you call to me, call to me'.

She climbed down and reached it. It was an old postcard. There was only one sentence: 'So sorry. It's better this way.' Then one kiss, and no signature. Savage, she smiled, worse than getting dumped by text! Addressed to Giles, in Chiswick, no postcode, dated July 1990. On the front was a beach and the words *Valencia, Spain* in bright yellow. Perfect – this was perfect. She held it up by its edges like an artefact, framed it with her fingers. She slid it into the back pocket of her jeans. This was the funny thing about people, Ashleigh had learnt, and it kept getting more true. The funny thing was that the more people had, the less they knew about what was there. They actually had no idea.

Maybe she would go to Spain one day. Dump some guy from there. She sat down on the chair and went back to the poem, his breakup soundtrack. Someone in an 'air-blue gown'? She imagined the woman as a balloon floating away over the horizon. Away to Valencia. 'Wistlessness...' 'Wind oozing...' The words made Ashleigh shiver. She mouthed them again.

She flipped back a few pages and hovered over the lines:

> Like that wound of mine
> Of which none knew,
> For I'd given no sign
> That it pierced me through.

Everything went quiet inside her. Ashleigh read the lines through again, her mouth slightly open. When she had stared for a long time and memorised its author she slowly climbed back up to replace the book. She then pushed the chair back to its place, then came again and gazed up at all these books, so many, she ran a hand along the worldly, mesmerising shelves.

18

TARA READS

Book club was round at Stacey's place tonight. Tara had entered into battle with Charlotte over who was going to get Ashleigh to babysit. Tara won by saying how traumatic the sacking of Samina had been and that Betsy was still beside herself about it. Tara smiled at the memory – back off Charlotte! I didn't get a career in TV by being a pushover did I, she thought, why the hell should I be nice? That was basically the problem with women, always trying to be liked.

It was the same old mums plus that one who'd come once before, Pratiksha. They'd done a run of slightly-too-long historical tomes and even some works in translation, then more recently some thrillers with 'girl' in the title. Tonight's book, *The Help*, was, for Tara, firmly inside the consciousness-raising category. She reached out her glass for the chilled wine and set the evening in motion by announcing that she'd read it too quickly, 'I try to slow myself down, but it's hard—'

Stacey held up an interrupting hand, 'I've got two different ways of reading: nibble or devour,' she paused and looked left to right. 'Devouring is when you're on holiday – I got through four books in Chamonix. But nibbling is bit by bit. It's like eating chocolates: you either make the box last, or you eat the whole lot.'

'Obviously eat the whole lot,' someone shouted.

'But seriously, though,' Stacey held her wine glass by the stem and gestured in the air, 'if you make them last by having one chocolate every day, that makes you fatter.'

Silence.

'Stacey,' said Tara, 'it's the exact same number of calories.'

Stacey looked from side to side, laughing. 'No, but if you eat one a day then they're, like, inside you for longer. Books are the same. So nibbling, you know, stretching it out, it's better. You get more... book vitamins. Like figuratively, I mean, obviously.'

Stacey looked round the table of incredulous faces, flustered.

'Anyway, what did the rest of you think of it?'

'Well, I read it on the Tube but kept getting the characters mixed up, so I ended up reading the same bit four times over.'

'Wait, does that count as constipation?'

Everyone sniggered. The book failed to divide opinion in a productive way. Everyone agreed that it was really good and that racism was really bad and that bitchy mums were the worst, then moved straight on to school gossip. One of the blonde mums told how someone's son was going private for secondary but didn't see why people were so judgey about it because 'actually he got a scholarship'. She did quote-mark fingers. The other blonde mum said people's judginess was because that family wouldn't share their maths tutor.

Tara felt short-changed and tried to steer them back towards some key themes. She'd planned out her observations while reading, picking areas that would generate some heat. For starters: if we'd lived in those times, wouldn't we be racist too? And did it matter that the author was white? The latter met with general bafflement, someone said I don't even get the question, the writer's just doing her job.

CHAPTER 18

Pratiksha had been quiet up to this point but she tentatively put up a hand.

'Well, for your second point I think that authorship totally matters.' She cleared her throat and went on. 'It's not only about representation, it's also the issue of whose story this—'

Someone burst in: 'It's good to have a message, though. Our nanny got a series from the library called *Bedtime Bravery for Little Radicals* and it shows how Red Riding Hood is actually about menstrual taboo and that Goldie Locks symbolises British colonial rule.'

'So the three bears are, like, Africa?'

'No wait, but seriously,' another launched in, 'you know what we need more of in books – contraception! Not even joking, I had my coil fitted and it was like the GP was trying to ram a shovel up my fanny, and I literally thought, how come this never gets described in books?'

Pratiksha's words dangled unattended while people began instead to offer up literary heroines in need of an intrauterine device. Tess, Madame Bovary, Anna Karenina – set literature's women free with an IUD, and don't even get us started on equal pay and a room of our own!

More wine, more laughter. Tara felt the itching need to bring in a mention of her own work, her new secret obsession with writing a screenplay. Surely it was time to share the news. Since Giles hadn't been interested. This was a book club, after all! Shouldn't they care about writing? She began to craft it in her mind, breezy, as if it had just occurred to her to mention it.

The blonde mums were still at it. 'So I was like: when you say "actually he got a scholarship", you mean you "actually" applied for it first. They don't come and throw one at you in the frozen food aisle, you don't slip up in the street and go,

"Whoops! We're accidentally in private education!" What's that all about?'

'I don't see what's wrong with wanting the best for my children,' Charlotte said stiffly. 'I got into Oxford because my parents worked hard and made sacrifices to give me the education I needed to get me there!'

The blonde mums ignored her. 'They dish those scholarships out though – they're a made-up thing so people have an excuse: they can disguise it as specialness.'

A third mum joined the blonde fray, 'Oh my special, special child, my preciousss…' They started doing *Lord of the Rings* voices and one of them got wine up her nose.

Tara still couldn't quite find the right moment. She almost dived in, then surprised herself by shying away. Why was her heart racing? She moved the balloon-sized wine glass slightly to the side. Her hands were sweaty. It was warm, she flapped her T-shirt and looked around the room irritably as if to blame the furniture. Her eyes moved along, one book club member to the next, over their animated, booze-shining faces. God, they were boring.

19

ASHLEIGH ASKS

This was more fun – the underwear drawer; the number-one crime-scene investigation. Ashleigh was in the parental bedroom, playing a game of her own invention: Sporty or Skanky. She'd even made up a theme tune. The narrator voice came up: Will it be tidy white pants, or a tangle of twisted thongs? Once she found a dirty pair, crunchily twisted around a panty-liner covered in brown blood. Seriously. But these were looking good. Bright colours: purple, blue and red. Silky-looking. No M&S six-packs and not a thong in sight. Ashleigh checked the gusset: no stains. Calvin Klein! She held them approvingly over her own body before folding and putting them back.

His drawer was boring, apart from his boxers were completely identical. She checked right to the back: all the exact same blue. The label: Jermyn's, Bond Street. This placed him way down the Men's Underwear League. So this was where his junk nestled all day long. She hooked her fingers into the waistband and lifted a pair up to her face, pulsing them in front of her open mouth, briefly miming a blowjob. Then she stretched and pinged them so they flew over the bed and landed in a heap. In your dreams, loser.

Underwear drawers were where people often hid their sex stuff. Condoms and all that. Sometimes she found sex toys which was gross. Once she had found one shaped like a huge dick, she sniffed it, it didn't smell of anything. She switched it on and left it buzzing away on the floor. She imagined them at it later, and what they'd do when their batteries went flat. But so far there was nothing like that here – not yet.

Sometimes she'd get herself off in people's beds. Rubbing between her legs, even just clamping her thighs together was enough sometimes. Thinking about her future self, Ms Hay, even Samina. She lay back with a sigh, seeking out those thoughts. She closed her eyes and touched her nipples in turn, waiting to see if they would harden. 'Bare cock!' The memory of getting shoved against the corridor wall pushed into her mind. 'She just wants bare cock!' The same boys who sat behind her in history sharing videos of a woman getting it from six men. Ashleigh opened her eyes to shake that thought away. She pulled her hands out from under her clothes and rolled angrily on to her side.

She pushed herself back up on their bed next to the discarded underpants. She lifted each pillow in turn, pressed her face into it and inhaled deeply. Hers was nicer, as you'd expect, but his wasn't all that bad. Not too scalpy, fairly fresh. She smoothed the pillows with precision, and carefully returned the underpants. Then she sat down again and paused for a while before picking out and rolling a dry bogey from her left nostril. She placed it between their pillows. 'Plausible deniability,' she said out loud – a phrase she'd recently overheard.

Swinging her legs she sat and thought for a while, looking around. On each side of the bed was a small chest of drawers. At the back of one of the drawers she found something new: a rolled up piece of paper wrapped around a box labelled Cyclogest. The medications in Ashleigh's other homes were straight forward: anti-depressants, anti-allergens and Cal-Pol. Stacey's bathroom harboured a treasure-chest of laxatives: bulk-forming, osmotic and stimulant.

But this was something she'd never seen before. She shook out a plastic strip of large individual bullet-shaped tablets. 'Cy...clo...gest...' she murmured, unravelling the paper booklet inside, frowning. She turned the box over and read the back out loud: Pessaries for Vaginal or Rectal Use. *Make your mind up – front door or back?* She held it up and pulled a tragic loser face. The audience lost it.

So were they trying for another baby? Now she thought of it, she had never found evidence here of any contraceptives. She made a note to extend this line of inquiry into the vitamins and supplements downstairs. She thought about the heaps of toys stacked around Betsy's solitary bed. How weird not to have siblings. Even shit ones like Morgan. Yes, these guys should totally have another kid, she decided. It would take some posh-parent heat off poor Betsy. She looked again at the pessaries and imagined their journey into Tara. Three had already been used. Good luck, she whispered theatrically to them as she returned them to their box and back into the drawer.

Over on the man's side was a tidy landscape of a lamp, a box of tissues, an asthma inhaler and *Phantom* by Jo Nesbø. She picked the book up and felt it was bulging slightly. She flicked it open. A paper bag was stuffed between its back pages. Right, OK. Inside were two very small plastic bags. Yes. One was half full of white powder. The other was empty. There was also a tiny plastic strip of tablets, several were popped open in an insultingly random way. The pills had no branding or label.

She should've predicted this, with his hair and his Converse, his pathetic 'I've still got it' cool-dad vibe. She smiled to herself. Are you kidding? It really was unbelievable that there had once been a theory called penis envy. She measured out a tiny quantity of the powder on to the palm of her hand. She touched her tongue to it. It had a bitter, ear-wax taste. She wrapped it up in one of his tissues and tucked it in her pocket. She might put it into their Greek yoghurt.

She stood, buoyed up on these new discoveries. The narrator voice was delighted with her – in its finest gameshow tones: *Another breakthrough – how does she do it?* In the corner of the bedroom was a leather swivel chair with a few silken scarves draped across its back. She padded across the shaggy carpet, sat down in the chair and swung herself from side to side with her feet planted on the floor.

'I'm glad you asked,' she replied.

Back into her science reporter voice, Ashleigh recited the seven steps of the scientific method:

1. Question,
2. Hypothesis,
3. Prediction,
4. Testing,
5. Analysis,
6. Replicate,
7. Share results.

Then back inside her head she ran through them again, but with less swagger. It was easy enough to replicate her work, she repeated the same investigations in all her different homes. Again and again. But final step – the sharing? Impossible. There was no one to share it with. The thrill of her druggy discoveries faded. She sighed, stood up and wandered back through into the gleaming bathroom, closed the toilet seat and sat down on top. She saw her reflection in the mirror. Her posture was slumped and her eyes looked smudged.

She knew she couldn't share, that was obvious, but there was another nagging feeling. She was troubled by a sense that her work wasn't... perfect. Perfect as in its original meaning of completed, finished. That's what she wanted. It wasn't only Step 7, Step 1 was missing too... The question. It was always changing. Why did she do it? What was the question – the actual question? This was the other flaw in her scientific method. It was a new question every time. Or maybe it wasn't. What was the question?

She looked at herself in the warmly lit mirror, around the gleaming room and back to herself, and then spoke out loud: 'Why do you have all this, and not me?'

20

TARA CAN'T BE ARSED

Tara decided she should start by talking about the author then steer the conversation towards her own experiences of writing. Or maybe she should bring the conversation back to the book, and to herself from there? No one cared about the bloody book any more though. Look at them, chewing, gulping, wittering away. Her stomach twisted. What kind of book club was this anyway? Finally the moment came, a medium-sized pause when seconds of the parmigiana were going round, so she cleared her throat and projected:

'So, I'm writing something myself. It's development for a screenplay based on that blog, the FGM blog?'

She twirled a strand of her hair.

'I… I've been working on it whenever I can, but it's hard, you know with Betsy – childcare – it's like I can never quite get the time…'

'That's what CBeebies is for, isn't it!' someone laughed. And right there the chat was drawn like a magnet straight back to kids, and kids' TV, and the immortal topic of screen time, how much and how often. Tara didn't join in. She felt a slackening feeling and moved the waistband of her Paige jeans. What on earth had got her so tongue-tied? She swigged at her wine as her frustration grew.

'Yeah, and some of those hot dads who read the *Bedtime Hour*,' Charlotte cackled. 'I won't say no!'

'It's nearly always a black dad reading,' Stacey mused. 'I mean, like, way more than you see at school. Is it like – a role model thing? Have you noticed that?'

Tara saw Pratiksha roll her eyes and take a deep breath. She'd fallen quiet since her previous point but was clearly preparing to speak up again: 'First of all, the school gate isn't exactly teeming with white dads either,' she said. 'But secondly I think there's a really important question around diversity and role models, actually—'

'What's so special about dads, anyway?' interrupted Tara, weighing in out of sheer irritation. 'Since when was being male enough to make you a role model?'

'Oh come on, it's good for men to read to children. How can you argue against that?' said Stacey. 'Otherwise it's more work for us when we could be uncorking another one of these babies.' She reached across for the chilled bottle of Pouilly Fuissé Burgundy, refilled her own glass then poured it round.

'But role models really do matter!' Pratiksha tried again. 'You British still have no idea about what diversity even—'

'Oh god, that's so American,' said Tara. 'You're all so PC.'

'Yeah, and anyway, you're like, Asian – you know, Brown. You guys are really successful,' added Stacey. 'Look at politics. Doctors. Asians all over the place. You guys don't need a special slot reading the bedtime story on children's TV, do you?'

'Wait – what!' Pratiksha's eyes flashed. 'OK, this isn't about me, I'm just saying—'

'Saying it should be a rainbow society. Like all the assemblies at school. But does it achieve anything?' Stacey stared around, challenging the table. 'The Muslim girls still won't come on play dates even if they all sing anti-bullying songs every day.'

'Are you seriously suggesting we shouldn't teach kids about racism?' Pratiksha was slack-jawed.

'All I'm saying is, there's no point,' Stacey waved her wine glass, 'if people don't want to integrate. I've invited Orson's whole class and Hugo's whole class and it's always the same kids who don't show up. And I'm sorry, but they're the Muslims. They just are. Talking about racism doesn't make me the racist!' she concluded, with her eyes slightly more wide open than they needed to be.

Tara yawned widely. It was enough to make her wish she could be a Muslim kid and not have to be here listening to Stacey's bullshit. My Orson this, my Hugo that, she would throw up if she heard any more about Stacey's kids. She'd looked in Hugo's bookbag and his reading level was higher than Betsy's when everyone said boys were supposed to be further behind in literacy. Tara sighed.

'Well, I'm not racist,' the Gollum-impersonating mum said.

Got to hand it to her, though, Tara thought, this wine is bloody good, and she drained the glass.

'No, god, no, me neither,' said her friend.

There was an awkward pause. Tara looked up. Typical bloody Stacey – she'd gone too far again. People glanced at each other and then everyone looked at Pratiksha. Pratiksha sat straight with a tight smile, and took a breath: 'So apparently I speak for London's Muslims despite being an American Sikh. OK. Does it suit you to know that it's the Bangladeshi kids who are responsible for rising school grades in London? They are the ones generating improved school reports. They are pushing up your house prices. That's your

Muslims. Although what this has to do with me I have literally no idea.'

'She's right, you know,' Tara announced. There was another pause. She nudged her empty wine glass towards Stacey's proffered bottle and then tilted her head to show that this was not an easy piece of wisdom to share. 'White kids are hopeless these days. I mean – the, you know, underprivileged ones.'

They all began jabbering over each other at once. 'No, the eastern Europeans do well, Polish and so on, and they're white – it's the natives who are failing!'

'What about Ashleigh the babysitter, though! Straight-A genius, apparently.'

'And when you think about her background, god!'

'But her little sister Morgan – she's in Orson's class and she still holds the pencil in her fist.'

'Oh, she came on our swimming party, and what's his name, the dad, he insisted on giving money for her ticket! It was funny, because obviously no one else paid.'

'Didn't their mum, like, kill herself?'

'Oh, I thought it was drugs, wasn't it?'

'God, poor kids!'

'Lily-Mae was invited to Morgan's party, but I found out they were going to McDonalds!'

The flurry calmed down again. Stacey smiled and looked around, feeling vindicated by the wave of responses. Pratiksha was silent, though. She took a sip of wine and wiped her eyes with the back of her hand. This movement triggered more glances. No one had noticed until this point that she was holding back tears. The glow from their jaunty foray into politics faded as the realisation spread that Pratiksha was upset, although no one was quite sure why.

'Hey, are you OK?'

'You know,' Pratiksha blinked. 'I faced racism growing up in the US because I wasn't American enough. And now I come here and I'm too American.'

'Oh right. So it's about being too American, rather than, you know… colour,' Stacey said, and looked defiantly at Tara. 'So at least it's not, you know—'

'No, it's just you—' Pratiksha stopped herself, then shook her head. 'I really try. But you guys can't even be bothered to pronounce my name.' She wiped at her cheek.

'Oh come on, it's supposed to be a book club, not a book blub,' Tara laughed loudly.

Stacey checked her phone, which made everyone else check their phones, and a collective murmur spread round about how late it had got. Stacey jumped up and offered teas and coffees that were drunk quickly through awkward pauses. Pratiksha was the first to leave. She picked up her bag and coat with her eyes down, and said a brief thank you on the way out. The door clicked closed after her, and there was a lull.

'Oh my god! What was all that about?'

'Since when was freedom of speech an issue in book clubs – what the hell!'

'Well she's a bit of a dark horse, isn't she. Oh wait – is that racist?' said Tara, to shrieks of relieved laughter. She'd steered the evening back on course and felt magnanimous. To lift the mood even more she related a story she'd been saving up. It was about how she'd gone for a facial the week before. It was supposed to be a Zen Deep Relaxation, 'But the girl scrubbed my face so hard, all the exfoliating stuff went in my eyes and up my nose, and when I shouted at her it got in my mouth too. So there she is, peeping over her little mask going, "Sorry ma'am, sorry ma'am—"'

'Was this on Finchley Road? Because I got a pedi up there,' Stacey cut in. 'I swear to god, she got out that razor blade thing, the potato peeler – she only went and sliced a chunk out of my heel. Blood everywhere!'

Everyone screamed in sympathy. But Tara hadn't had time to get to the funny part – Giles had loved it – where she sat up, wiped her face and handed the towel to the mask-peeping girl, then gone straight to the manager: 'She should get a job scrubbing floors, not faces!'

But anyway. She noted the rocket leaf stuck between Stacey's teeth as she leant back and tossed down the last of her wine. Let Stacey have her moment, she thought. Seriously, though, some people were so competitive.

21

ASHLEIGH CAN'T HELP HERSELF

Ashleigh left her drugs and her scientific theories behind and came downstairs. The front room curtains were closed over the bay window, encircling the rocking horse that Betsy said no one was allowed to ride. Ashleigh sat down on it, and it creaked loudly; she jumped off. She stood and looked through to the kitchen table, where her schoolwork was all set out. Her GCSEs were starting in under two weeks, but she'd finished all the past papers ages ago and been working above her grades all year. The situation didn't exactly represent a challenge to her. Ashleigh realised the absence of stress about them was maybe a bit sad. It wasn't stress, exactly, that she was after. It was just like she'd gone beyond this and got bored.

Maybe she should go through the family photos. There was a canvas series here: Betsy as a toddler dressed up as a daffodil, then she was a lion staring out from beneath a large golden mane, finally a bumble bee, her face like thunder. Ashleigh lifted each one, turned and examined then carefully replaced it. A while ago in another home Ashleigh had opened the backs of some framed photos. Behind one of the images on display she had discovered an older photo, hidden. A different child. She still hadn't solved that mystery, despite several deep searches.

So now she always checked, just in case. The canvas ones had nothing of course. But these other frames clicked open easily as she checked behind them, one by one. Next was a picture with both parents proudly holding their small daughter aloft. It reminded Ashleigh of footballers holding up a trophy, wrestling each other to try to be the one who's holding it the most. She quietly sang the *Lion King* theme as she moved on. Tropical holidays, nice cars, sunglasses and cocktails. The same poses again and again, like a celebrity timeline but with old people.

Dad had once told them about his mum. He never talked about family so she and Morgan paid attention. She was a hard woman, but liked everything frilly – it was funny, he said, she would disguise the toilet roll using a doll in a yellow dress. It stood staring at you on the bog, Dad said, its legs down the middle of the roll and the dress covering it all over. So even she was hiding something.

The family gallery continued in rows all the way up to the picture rail near the ceiling. One after another she unhooked them, turned them over to examine the backs, opened, checked and replaced them. The last one was higher up and hardest to reach. She carried a chair over and climbed up to reach it. But like the others, it had no secrets to reveal. She tried to hang it back up, holding the frame in both hands and dragging it over the hook. It failed to catch.

Holding the frame carefully Ashleigh climbed back down and pulled the chair closer to the shelving units alongside the fireplace. Frowning, she climbed back up again. Heaps of magazines lay on the shelf, one had Syrian refugees on the cover, another was headlined Duck-Egg Blue for Ever! She scowled. Who's ever seen a duck's egg? She pushed them aside so her foot fitted in and she could reach further up, balancing there with one leg on the chair and the other on the shelf. She was reaching up with the frame in both hands when a voice piped up behind her: 'What are you doing?'

She span round and nearly lost her balance. There in the doorway was Betsy.

'You're up. You should be in bed!' Ashleigh's face flushed.

Betsy looked pale and sleepy. She was twisting the back of her hair with one hand and staring at Ashleigh. She looked somehow blank, as though she might be sleep-walking.

'What… why are you looking?

Ashleigh composed herself. 'Just straightening it up,' she said. 'This picture was a bit wonky!' She smiled warmly to cover up the rushing feelings inside her and carefully stepped down from the chair.

'But… you took it down. Why are you watching our photos and not the TV?'

'Well, Betsy, I was bored without you. And everyone knows pictures are more interesting than TV. And books even more so,' her voice was bright and too sugary. 'So shall we read *What Do* again and get you back into bed? What are you up to, anyway! Come on, let's go…'

As she gabbled she realised this was the wrong pitch. Betsy wasn't like the others.

The child stood there frowning, and repeated her question in a more suspicious voice. 'Why, why are you looking?'

Ashleigh had to do better. She put the picture down. She moved towards the door, sat down on the floor and patted the carpet, gesturing for Betsy to join her there. Her mind was whirring and not in a way she enjoyed. She felt a completely unfamiliar weakness. This had never happened before. How had she let this happen? Betsy came and sat down next to her. To buy some time Ashleigh asked was she cold, did she want a blanket? Betsy shook her head and carried on looking at Ashleigh.

'OK. So. What am I doing? Betsy, I am doing Science. You can help me. How do we know this is real? How do we know you're not dreaming right now? I mean, it makes sense – you were in bed – I know because I put you there. So maybe this is a dream.'

'But it's not.'

'But how can you prove it?' said Ashleigh. They sat together, side by side, their backs to the wall. She reached out and touched the glossy skirting board. 'This – this shiny paint, this soft carpet... What if it's all a dream?'

Betsy followed Ashleigh's touch, running her own small finger along the smooth paintwork.

'Well, what if you give me something,' said Betsy slowly, 'a thing which I can keep in my hand, and then it'll still be there in the morning?'

'But what does that prove?' Ashleigh replied gently. 'I mean, tomorrow morning when you still have the thing, that could be part of the dream too?'

'And maybe you might take it off me when I go to sleep,' Betsy's voice was reproachful as she caught hold of the bottom of her sleeve, rolling and twisting the fabric. She was looking down and Ashleigh couldn't see her face, only her hair all fuzzed up at the back. 'And that's not fair, and anyway, why were you on top of a chair?'

Ashleigh couldn't help smiling at this. As a babysitter she technically qualified as an old person, but she swore never to use their tactics. Never. She would never say 'because I said so' or tell a young person to stop asking questions. That was old person bullshit. *Refusal to tolerate free inquiry*. She'd be betraying her own self if she did that. Dad once shouted at her: 'You've got an answer for every bloody thing, you.' Her triumphant reply: 'No, I've got a question for every bloody thing!' Dad had whacked her.

Ashleigh slumped down the wall. She felt slack, humbled. It was almost a feeling of relief. She took in a large breath.

'OK, Betsy, I will tell you. I was looking for – something. Something that belongs to me, but I can never find it. I don't know. But I keep looking.'

She rubbed her eyes. Betsy looked up at her.

'It's… I'm trying,' her voice went higher and faded. 'I can't stop myself.'

She avoided the child's steady gaze, leaning her head forward to rest her chin on her knee. She stared at the floor between their legs. She sniffed, and swallowed, and blinked.

'And that's the truth, and it sounds slanted and tricky, but that's probably what truth is like anyway.' She pressed her fingers and then her palm into the thick pile of the carpet, pushing the fibres backwards and forwards. 'And I'm only telling you because you're clever and not stupid like most people.'

There wasn't anything else Ashleigh could say. Then Betsy did a strange thing. She reached out and took Ashleigh's hand, and held it tightly between both of hers. They didn't look at each other.

22

TARA SQUATS

Tara pushed the front door open and took her jacket off in the hall. She looked in the door – there was Ashleigh, working away at the kitchen table. Tara came in.

'How was it?'

'Fine! All good, she was so good.' Ashleigh stood up and slid her work into her bag on the table. 'OK, if you need me this week just message me.'

'Great. Here,' Tara had the cash ready, 'Rounding up to 11 p.m. even though it's only quarter to!' She smiled magnanimously. Ashleigh smiled back, folded the cash into the pocket of her bag, stood up and made straight for the door. This was just right – Tara couldn't stand it when people took ages and she had to make small talk. It was intuitive the way Ashleigh knew just to pack and leave. The front door clicked behind her.

Tara sat down heavily on the sofa. She wished Giles would come back from the pub, so she could complain about Stacey, and he'd definitely agree because Stacey's husband had once got drunk and told Giles that journalists were a bunch of in-bred ponces who all lived in cloud cuckoo land. She really only stayed friends with her because of school. She should ditch this book club and start a new one. A proper book club, with interesting people – maybe from her old work. Anything to get away from hearing about other people's children and Stacey's incomprehensible chocolate theories.

She stood up and moved into the kitchen area. She saw herself reflected in the sliding doors. She stood taller and pulled her belly in. She lowered her chin. Were the eye-bags worse? She pressed her fingers into her stomach and then clenched her abs to expel them. Then the muffin-top manoeuvre: lifting the waist of her jeans up and over. All good. Seriously, not bad. Especially for a mum. Hot Trainer had paid off. Shame about the whole sacking thing but it served him right for using her photo on his website. Bloody cheek, lucky he didn't get sued.

She turned sideways and put her shoulders back, still looking at herself, shook her hair down and then tied it back up. She rinsed the dishes and cups that were in the sink and loaded them into the dishwasher. Some leaves had collected in the plug. Rocket leaves, the most perseverant, most inde-structible of leaves. Stacey had looked such an idiot trying to show off with salad on her teeth like that, Tara smiled. Rocket – now that stuff's invincible, lasts five rounds in a dishwasher. She shook the leaves into the food waste caddy. Did it persist the same way in intestines, she wondered?

Tara had a vague fear, a recurring day-mare about her own guts. The fear was that deep inside she resembled tinned dog food from an old TV advert. 'Meaty chunks in jelly.' Even the idea of the smell appalled her. She had browsed the Goop website and considered trying to ban white food until Giles teased her about it. She'd read about faecal trans-plantation but knew she couldn't take it further without him finding out. But how else to get a colon like Gwyneth's? She sighed, standing there, one hand on the kitchen side and one hand on her hip.

CHAPTER 22

How could a book club make you feel even more lonely than you already were? If Giles was here, they'd be on the same side and she'd be more herself. Her idea of herself was that she demonstrated strength in front of her husband. So much so that now she wasn't sure how not to. 'I've got no problem with women in authority,' he'd say. 'I'm used to it.' He liked saying how tough Tara had been in pregnancy and birth. She knew these comments reflected well on her, she basked in them. She silently wished they were true.

All the time she'd been resisting the idea of another baby, she also feared the possibility of not being able to have one if she chose to. She told herself that the Cyclogest experiment was just to have it as an option, so she could then rule it out. Maybe. Or maybe she should just give up and have another one? The thought slipped out that it'd be nice to have a civilised one that didn't bite, and she immediately felt ashamed. Poor Betsy.

She looked at her phone once more and decided not to message Giles again. She'd go to bed alone. But before heading up she jumped up and down a few times in the kitchen to try to settle her tummy. She squatted down with a grunt, then did a few star jumps, holding on to her breasts because of her flimsy bra. There was no getting around it, and she could no longer blame it on their homemade Paleo breakfast granola, Tara suffered from trapped wind.

Night after night she felt the cursed bubbles moving down her bowels. Sometimes she raised a buttock, allowing the gas to emerge soundlessly. But this was high-risk, she once misjudged and let rip a beast in their marital bed. Giles screamed that he would rather die than have a wife who farted like a long-distance trucker and if she did it again they would sleep in separate rooms for ever. She feigned laughing it off, saying she was blasting the patriarchy and he'd better watch out.

She tried to self-medicate. She guzzled down the Gaviscon and the Rennies Deflatine, plus the Ayurvedic tea hidden in her make-up bag. Nothing seemed to work though. She sighed, and look again at the mirror. She did a few more jumps, jostled the last of the cups into the dishwasher and set it off with a quiet hum. The house was still. Her phone had no new messages, Giles hadn't answered her last one about when he was coming home. She bent down into a squat one last time, then straightened up and set off upstairs. She'd just have to keep farting in secret.

23

LUDI CAN'T HELP ASHLEIGH

Ludi was making toast and Morgan was eating her cereal. Ash was stood by the table. It was unusual that they were together at the same time in the kitchen area, Ash was usually gone by now. Morgan's spoon clinked in her bowl and Ludi started to butter the toast. Ash was looking at her phone. Suddenly out of nowhere she spoke. 'That jam, it's so cheap,' she nodded her head towards the table. 'You can tell by the colour.'

Ludi tried to laugh, 'What the hell's a cheap colour?

'You can see the cheapness!' she sneered. 'Dad's gone to Iceland!'

Morgan looked up from her half-empty cereal bowl at Ashleigh, then at him, and quickly back down at her bowl again. 'Sorry, Your Highness,' he tried to do a jokey face for Morgan's benefit, 'I'll make sure it's organic Marks and Spencer's whatevers next time.'

'Seriously, though, look,' and this time she blew up. 'SuperValu? They can't even afford to spell it!' She snatched up the cereal box from in front of Morgan's face and shook it at Ludi. 'They can't afford an "e"? Tara would rather DIE than let her kid eat junk food. She actually said that. And look what we get – food for people who can't spell!'

As Ash ranted, he saw Morgan flinch. Her face looked like she was wondering, What is this – is something wrong with us? Like she might cry, scared by that rage. And he couldn't bear any more fear in the house – after all they'd gone through, to still have fear. He couldn't bear it.

He tried to stop himself, tried to keep control, but he couldn't.

Later on he was walking Morgan in to school and he felt bad. He wished that he hadn't told Ashleigh to fuck off and live in Tara's house if Tara was so fucking great. Morgan was quiet for most of the way and then on the last block she said she wanted to walk to school on her own.

Then he felt even worse. He watched her go, stood there like an old saddo, then turned to walk back home. He hated himself. Maybe he hated Ashleigh too. Maybe she was no better than her mum. Her face came into his mind, her scornful face. He tried to see her baby face, when she was soft. When she first started school, and she used to hold on to his hand when he dropped her off on his way to work.

Back then he just wanted to be out the house, Morgan was on the way by now, Diane hated being pregnant, wouldn't look after herself, what was the point, she'd say. Back then, when it was getting worse. Ludi got the sliding feeling. Diane had the thing about the bathroom floor. When anyone got out the bath they had to be stood on a towel and not make any wet patches. Even though he got a bath mat from Argos. (Bright yellow – what happened to that?) But she didn't want that wet either, even though that's what it was for.

One time Ashleigh jumped out the bath and ran to get her penguin towel instead. Left a little trail of bathwater. He heard it from the kitchen – Diane flipped, out the blue. He ran, then he stopped. There she was towering over Ashleigh like a giant pregnant raging monster. Screaming. Ash's small little body, rooted to the spot. The bubbles from the bubble bath still sliding down her legs. The wet footsteps on the floor. And him, frozen, not moving.

When this sight came into his mind it pushed a sound out of Ludi's throat that he couldn't stop. He gulped it back down, keeping it down with the deep tears. Right there in the street the old feelings came. Bubbles on the back of her little skinny legs. Ludi gulped again and a tear escaped from his eye, it went in a hot flow down his cheek. He didn't stop or wipe his face, as more tears poured and poured down, one straight after the other without stopping. Off his chin and on to his neck.

Diane had left them just after Morgan was born. He stopped himself from thinking about it a long time ago and he never talked about it. It was behind him now. He didn't even think about it. Never. But what did he have to lose? So. The mother of his children went away. Like he said she escaped from them, instead of the other way round. These days you were meant to call it depression or whatever, but everyone just said she was a psycho. Scabby Mark went round telling everyone, even in Londis. Ludi clenched his fists. That scabby-eyed cunt had the nerve to come round the same month asking for money she owed.

Ludi pulled himself onwards as though he was fighting gravity. Diane left them. It still seemed impossible. He had never found the words to explain it. He stopped and pushed the heels of his hands into his eye sockets. He breathed out and rubbed his face. Maybe Ashleigh did remember. He was wrong, he did have something to lose. He couldn't lose Ashleigh. What if she remembered? Maybe he should've told the truth.

24

TARA CAN'T HELP HERSELF

It was a buzzing work day and Tara was staring into her old editor's glass office. It was in the corner of a much larger open office space, full of bright screens and even brighter people. She could feel it in her veins. She'd spent years here – she had become herself right here. The loneliness of book club had spurred her into action. Over two days she had worked up the precise level of breeziness before calling him on the phone. 'Hey! It's been ages! I'm coming by the office tomorrow for a couple of other meetings anyway – can I drop in for a quick hello?'

The plan was to sound him out about job-share or part-time work, in an unofficial way. This used to be inconceivable in the TV world, but times were definitely changing. Flexible working and job-sharing – it was everywhere now. She might drop a few ideas, a positive Syrian refugee story, maybe a heroic FGM campaigner. She might even mention her screenplay too. Got to get back in the mix, she told herself. Times may be changing, but nets still had to be worked.

Tara would never admit it, but she knew Giles was right. About the work thing. But not about their huge fight after she'd sacked the bloody nanny though. Because even if she had overreacted a bit, the police even weren't that interested. She'd decided not to press charges as long as Samina was given a warning. There was something called a harassment warning. Basically it wouldn't come to anything, and Tara was relieved it was all over. Betsy was doing tennis school this summer, and they had Ashleigh. And now she was here, wearing proper clothes, shaking things up on the work front. So it was all good.

Here, back in the very heart of work-land, all pumped up and ready to shine. The sea of screens stretched away in every direction, the overheads showing all the different feeds and channels. It was like being at the heart of a complex ecosystem, it was thrilling. She inhaled the power, the work memories, the deep pulse of her old life. At the same time, as she looked out over the room she began to feel weirdly invisible, as though she was behind a one-way mirror.

Tara glanced back into her editor's glass office. He clocked her, looking up from his phone conversation and doing a 'in a minute' wristwatch gesture which she answered with a bright smile. Here on the outside, the air was hot. She looked round, maintaining the smile even though there was no one here she knew. She stepped to the side and her shin bumped against a low chair. 'Oh – oops!' she said out loud, to no one. She adopted a power stance, phone in hand, as if to suggest a stream of urgent communications. She refreshed all her media – no notifications, no messages.

She was standing and scrolling through some recent photos when a voice made her jump.

'Admiring your kids?'

Tara flinched and snapped her phone off. There at her side was Vedhika, glossy as ever, one of those unstoppable young achievers. She'd never been on Tara's team but had once asked for advice on a promotion. Tara had been insanely busy at the time. Well she certainly seemed to be doing all right for herself now, with all that bouncing black hair, and her jeans and Converse. Tara regretted her leather skirt and boots.

'Oh, Vedhika, hi! I've got a meeting actually,' she nodded her head towards the glass door, behind which the editor was firmly on his phone and still hadn't turned around. 'So, are you still an AP?'

'Er, no! I've been a producer for two years now. And you – how many kids are you up to?

'Just the one – that's enough for me, haha!'

'Sweet,' said Vedhika, and smiled patiently. There was a pause and then they both spoke at once.

'That's great!—'

'—OK, got to dash!'

Vedhika went and joined a group clustered around a monitor, all talking excitedly. Others moved around without a glance in her direction. Tara cleared her throat, moved her weight from one booted foot to the other, then checked the time on her phone. It was ten minutes after the time they'd agreed. Fifteen since she'd arrived outside her editor's door. Her armpits were sweaty and she felt an urgent need to rush home and into her friendly old tracksuit bottoms. The editor finally put down the phone, stood up and pulled his door wide open.

'Tara! Come in!'

Six minutes later Tara was back outside the editor's door again, loudly wishing him all the best as she pulled it closed and turned to leave. The wide smile deflated as she moved away without looking up once. She took the stairs down and rushed past the reception, handing her guest ID pass back in without a word. She shot outside into the air and regained her breath. It was a grey morning. She was outside again.

Back outside in the world of loser people with no jobs. Grey sky, grey air, even the trees were as colourless as fruit salad on a plane.

This had been a mistake. This had been horrible. Beyond horrible. He had boasted on and on about his latest awards and audience figures. She had smiled until her cheeks hurt. She hadn't told him about her screenplay. She hadn't told him that times were definitely changing or that flexible working was everywhere now. She had just about managed to say she'd be very happy to consider a job-share, in case anyone else was asking, and he'd said 'Great idea – you'll be the first to know!' and looked at his watch.

Tara chewed the insides of her cheeks. She frowned, thinking plenty of women with kids seem to find their way back into their lives again. Why the hell can't I, she thought, when will it happen? What am I doing wrong? Should I just give in to Giles and have another one? Of course she loved Betsy, but she was six now! And Tara was ready to be something else. And she didn't see why no one else seemed to feel like this. No one else was saying this.

She wanted to work – she was trying. Couldn't he see? This wasn't who she was – she needed to be herself again. 'I know what I want!' As she whispered the words out loud her voice cracked and tears stung her eyes. Was it going to be this life now, was this it? She had ceased to be visible, she scarcely seemed to be audible. There were no traces of her old life, this new one had closed over it, swallowed it up like slick vinyl paint, there wasn't even so much as an outline. Her presence in the world was diminished. She wanted to erupt like a volcano, she wanted to take up space, to occupy the world. And why shouldn't she! But how?

131

She tried to be rational, to give herself advice. She lifted her head up, told herself: I am an ambitious woman and I make no apologies for it. Just keep up the exercise, less social media and more screenplay. Maybe more work on the FGM campaign. There was no knowing where it could lead. It would come round eventually. She had to take herself more seriously, like Giles said. Write some lists. It was all a matter of time. These were her wise words to herself. But they had no effect; it was like she was trying to tickle herself.

She headed back towards the station. There was still some afternoon left because Ashleigh was collecting Betsy from tennis. A breeze fluttered, the sun came out and shone on a cluster of small trees. It was a shame to waste the day. Tara paused outside a wide and brightly lit sports shop window. She looked in. Who could resist a sale on yoga pants? Pants – what a terrible word. But there they were, shining like slick balloons. And 40% off. She'd go in and try some on, just in case. Also: retail therapy. She laughed hollowly – she'd always wanted to kill women who used that phrase. Even more girly than 'me time'.

Scooping up an armful of slippery neon leggings Tara went to the changing rooms and took a large plastic number five from the assistant. He was tall with dark brown eyes. As she passed she held his gaze for a second. Maybe he thinks I'm a cougar, she smiled to herself. Of course she wasn't old enough. As he returned to hanging clothes on a rail she saw the muscles of his back moving under his T-shirt. Her lips smiled. The music was loud, and she quietly sang along. 'Fire away, fire away,' She felt better already. 'Fire away, fire away.'

Behind the cubicle door there were hairs on the floor and a clump of dust. She wrinkled her nose as she pulled off her boots and stripped down to her underwear, piling her clothes up on the bench. Her T-shirt had huge sweat patches under the arms. She leant, relieved, her hot skin against the coolness of the mirror. After a pause she turned her back to the full-length mirror and twisted to look over her shoulder at her bum. It looked good in these knickers. But turning back she felt a clot of blood slide warmly out – oh god, of course – her period, on top of everything else.

They'd got so much worse recently, she was using night-time pads during the day. She checked the so-called wings, they had bunched inwards and stuck to themselves. She coaxed them apart and re-stuck them round the edges of her knickers. Should be OK – at least until she got back home. Wings indeed, she thought, like my wings: clipped, bloody, useless. But at least it was an excuse to reject Giles and his tireless prodding.

She reached down into her bag for the Clarins lip gloss and applied it generously, licked her teeth, then pouted at herself from different angles. She shook her hair out of its pony tail and ran her hands down over her lacy bra. Her breasts were slightly swollen because of her period; the tenderness made them sensitive. A warm ache began between her legs. She turned and admired her backside again, arched her back a little, pulled her tummy in and raised one arm up. She looked really good. She imagined that dark-eyed assistant coming in, taking off his shirt, the mirrors...

But as she adjusted her pose again, a squeak cramped her guts. She frowned. Maybe it was period cramps, or the hangover of her nightly gas troubles. She twisted again the other way, trying to find relief, and then squatted down on the floor in frustration. Without warning a fart blew out, deep and forceful, ending in a quizzical squeak. Tara froze.

There was one long second of silence, then an explosion of suppressed laughter from outside the cubicle door, and silence again. Tara's skin prickled with rage, all down her chest and back. She slowly stood up straight and squared her shoulders, breathing deeply. Fine. OK. She scanned the ceiling for security cameras. She put her clothes back on, and then her boots. She deliberately pulled her hair back into a tight, high ponytail. She lifted her chin and stared directly in the mirror.

The yoga-wear fell to the floor in an electro-coloured pile as she marched outside. The assistant stood there, petrified mid-breath. She slammed the five on to the desk and surged onwards past him like a royal navy destroyer, straight over to the checkout.

'Who's the manager here?'

Two young women looked at each other, then without a word one of them reached for a push button on the counter, leant forward and pronounced over the tannoy: 'Vivek to sales, please, Vivek to sales, customer query.'

Tara stood tall, feet in parallel, firm to the core. She gathered herself up. A thin man came round the edge of the sock department and hurried towards the counter. Once safely lodged behind it, he leant his head back and looked at Tara. He had no lips and he spoke in a monotone: 'How may I be of assistance?'

'Hello Vivek,' she said, her voice acid. 'I'm lodging a complaint about the member of your staff in the changing rooms. He tried to spy on me. That's an offence. He gave the impression he was going to follow me into the cubicle. His behaviour was lewd and intimidating. Vivek, I want to know what your company policy is regarding sexually inappropriate behaviour.'

He blinked slowly, 'What?'

'Vivek, I expect to be fully apprised as to how you deal with this matter. Unless you want to hear from my lawyer. Here's my card.' Tara placed her card on the counter, showing her old job title. That's right: a national news channel, yes. Do not fucking mess with me. Her ponytail swished and her boots were loud as she span and walked out, the blood leaping inside her veins. Even if he hadn't tried it on, he probably wanted to – he looked the sort. She refined her anger, polished it. It's about time we all stood up to men like that, she told herself. Well, he picked on the wrong woman today. She felt like Uma Thurman in *Kill Bill*. She resisted the urge to blow smoke from the gun of her fingertips. YES.

PART TWO

'All crime in the end is the crime of the community.'

H.G. Wells

25

ASHLEIGH GOES TOO FAR

Summer holidays meant long days, sunny pavements, and rising levels of parental desperation. Ashleigh was ready. She knew where all the holiday play-schemes were, the tennis clubs, theatre groups and team sports. She'd checked the library noticeboards and spotted a new one, Future Leaders: Confidence Coaching. She laughed, she should launch her own business: Pay Top Dollar to Feel Like a Top Parent dot com. Her exams were over now and the results didn't come out until August so it was a kind of in-between time. But there was work to do.

On the street Ashleigh didn't move like other teenagers. She didn't hover or hang around, and she didn't gravitate into groups. She was wearing her new Air Max and it was like walking on air. Everyone else did less in the holidays, but not her. Lately she'd been even more awake at night, and waking early, reading before anyone else even woke up. It was evening now but the daylight would last for hours. She smiled back at people as she went. She'd grown up on this street after all, and it was still hers, in a way.

She shone a special look at Nicky's house, their old neighbour, the kind one. His home was dusty compared to the rest of the street. The garage door beside it looked abandoned. She smiled again, to herself this time. Then she opened the gate next door and turned into their little garden. She was her usual five minutes early arriving at Tara's house, but slowed on the garden path at the sound of screaming from inside. There was a fight going on. She stopped in front of the door. More screaming, the sound of it ran down her veins and she had to hold herself from reeling back.

'Just keep fucking spending it why don't you!'

They were just like everyone else then. She faltered a moment longer and then rang. Of course they were like everyone else. She stood there. It was one of the things her work demonstrated. No one could escape that. Her left knee shook, she leant on to the right one. It was an old feeling, rising up. Ashleigh observed this reaction inside her own body, tried to prevent it, push it back down. She lifted and opened up her bag as if to explore its contents. She checked her breathing. She arranged her face into a casual expression of thinking about her homework on a sunny evening.

Giles pulled the door open with a manic smile. 'Great to see you Ashleigh do come on in we won't be long!' There was no sign of Tara. Giles stomped around the kitchen without looking at her. 'Um,' he said, scratching his head and looking out of the window, 'do you want to sit down there while she gets Betsy settled?' Ashleigh picked the chair at the end of the table and got her books out in a steady and ordinary way. Giles sighed dramatically, sat down at the computer desk nearby and ruffled his hair with both hands. She glanced over and looked at the back of his head, she loved the vulnerable backs of people's heads. It's the one place that they can't see, but you can. Then, his monitor lit up. And her entire body thrilled, poised like a hunting cat, as Giles typed in his password, which she could clearly read: Betsy2006.

Her insides burst into flames as Ashleigh stared down at her books. Kid's name and year of birth – you have got to be kidding me. Her heart was pounding, was its beating visible? She kept her eyes down and unzipped her pencil case, gathered her face into a frown, and stared into the open pages of *To Kill a Mockingbird*. It opened directly to Calpurnia. She loved Calpurnia. Scout had no idea.

To add to the impression of deep concentration she narrowed her eyes, turned back a couple of pages, and made a tiny note in pencil beside the inner margin in immaculate handwriting that luckily Giles could not read because it said I've got you now, you dickhead. It was a long twenty minutes until Tara came down the stairs, her face tear-stained. Ashleigh avoided all but the briefest eye contact, her relaxed manner saying, Oh, I'd forgotten I was even in your house, this book's so fascinating. There was a brief exchange about what time they'd be back, then the couple left the house in silence. Ashleigh's mind had overruled that rinsing fear caused by the screaming. She now evaluated her response at 7% pity, 34% disgust and 59% who cares about your pathetic lives anyway. You're not special.

It was a challenge to her will power but Ashleigh knew she could do it. The desire to get logged into that computer was so strong, she was grinding her teeth. But she would save it, she would wait before she entered his computer and his inner life. She would take it slowly and do her regular research first. It was like a test – how long could she resist before logging in?

Filling in the customary ten minutes of desk-bound time, Ashleigh set out her other work in the correct order on the table. She'd brought history and physics. She reopened *Mockingbird* and turned back to the page she'd written on when she spied Giles' password. The narrator voice came up – *She's got her hands on the controls at last, ladies and gentlemen please prepare for lift-off.* She took her pencil and beneath her earlier comment she added the same phrase again and again, in the same small tidy writing, in a column:

I've got you
I've got you
I've got you
I've got you
I've got you
I've got you
I've got you
I've got you
I've got you
I've got you
I've got you
I've got you
I've got you
I've got you

all the way down the margin of the page. This historic triumph deserved to be revered, preserved, like an illuminated manuscript. She thought of the darkened rooms at the British Library where ancient pages lived below deep glass but shone through into her life. That was true history, the gathered-up power of the best thoughts humans had ever had, all in one place. The memory added to the swelling feeling. Ashleigh could feel her own power surging. She was unstoppable.

She stood up to move around, she needed to slow this reaction, it was happening too fast. Don't devour it! He'd made it too easy for her, she needed to slow herself down. She would make herself comb through at least two bookshelves before she did anything else tonight. She'd be thorough and stay in charge. It was two months since that night she'd been caught by Betsy, that had shaken her. She had promised herself to be more careful, she had to keep control.

The bedroom bookshelves didn't provide any new evidence but they gave back her feeling of discipline, of method. Even so Ashleigh kept feeling a fizzing, bubbling-over sensation, like a caffeine overdose. But in her mind. It was a crazier energy than she usually generated. The unopened computer was still waiting for her. She could feel something that was new, like a hormone pulsing inside her body.

She should check in on the medical drawers. Doing the rounds, she murmured, just doing my job. In her mind she smoothed down her white lab coat, beeped her secretary and told him to send in Mr and Mrs Birling: 'Dr Ashleigh Renton will see you now.' She watched them enter nervously, she took off her glasses and generously said 'Hello, Mr and Mrs Birling, please sit down – no, not there, right here opposite my desk. This won't take long. Looking at these blister packs, the dates show you haven't taken today's, have you?'

Playing out in the bathroom Ashleigh realised that she was still too excited. She knew why, of course: the computer password. But it wasn't good, this wasn't the correct way to begin a new investigation. Not many people could control themselves the way she could. She could even make herself blush if she stared in the mirror and focused hard enough. But now she needed to cool herself down, to get her focus back.

She moved on to the spare room, the one that used to be her family's kitchen. What would it give her? Since her first visit Ashleigh had persuaded herself that this space gave her something unique, that it had a presence, somehow meaningful for her. Today all she got was the memory of that burnt toast smell. It added on to Tara's screaming earlier, she felt suddenly poisoned. She didn't want to be in that room or in those memories any more. The thoughts she had been chasing after, they weren't welcome now.

She left, and carefully, very carefully, she opened Betsy's bedroom door. Silence. She moved soundlessly to the child's bedside and stood over her sleeping shape. She bent down and leant over to examine her face, her eye sockets, cheeks and still lips. She was much smaller than Morgan. She leant closer, nose to nose, so that their breath mingled. They were sharing the same oxygen, and the same place to be a small human being, safe from the world.

She felt a sharp urge to kiss her. She jolted back – what had got into her! She mustn't wake her, not with the computer still sitting unopened downstairs. She leant back. But that small nose, her resting eyelids – she was perfect like an angel; unknowing, untroubled by the shitty world of grown-ups. Homo sapiens but not too sapiens. On the opposite wall was a framed photo of baby Betsy sleeping on her front with her bum stuck up in the air. Ashleigh smiled. Morgan used to sleep like that.

It was ages since she'd looked up close like this at her own sister – usually she was trying to escape her. But the memory of that soft quiet breathing, and the peace; it touched her. And all the times she had tucked Morgan into bed, all the times she'd soothed her – they were still inside her.

She looked down at the child's miniature contours and imagined herself when she was this small. Suddenly her eyes blurred over. *No one did this for me. Watched me and leant over me. I was this small; I knew nothing.* Her mouth shook. Will I always be alone? *Ah, poor Ashleigh*, the narrator voice came in. *No!* She blocked it. No. She straightened up sharply and gulped. No tears, she told herself. God, she was getting out of control, even for her own self! No tears, she repeated, only anger. Calm, useful anger.

Ashleigh went back to the open door and hovered, still looking in. This quiet warm air contained a childish spell – it was hard to leave behind. But she wiped her eyes and inhaled, slowed her breath. Control, she was back in control. And, of course, there was work to do. She softly closed Betsy's door and began to make her way back down the stairs.

26

HOLLY DISCOVERS

It started so well, Holly's singing night. And that made it even worse. Normally she dropped Stanley round at Maureen's on the way down, and the community centre where they met for singing was close by so she could always get back in time. School was over for the summer and Stan was doing holiday club, which still felt wrong. The irony of putting her own kid in holiday club so she could go off and work in the Children's Social Care Unit! They joked about it at work.

Anyway, for her, singing night was almost like a holiday. It was a separate world, not connected to anything else she did. The rest of the group was a mix of retired people and younger women without kids, and they always went on to the pub afterwards. They had given up inviting her along, Holly was always the first to run off. But why shouldn't she go to the pub? First time in ages. The singing was the one and only selfish thing she had.

It still felt selfish though, reckless even, when she booked Ashleigh for the first time instead of asking Maureen. And not even for work – but just to go down the pub! She got the number off a Local Help postcard on the school pinboard. Ashleigh turned up early, chatted confidently, and got comfy with Stan by asking him about his mates in Year Two. And of course she knew them. Stanley was excited to have the same babysitter as Mimi and Orson and Betsy. Holly secretly laughed that she'd joined the Charlotte-Stacey-Tara school-gate elite by stealth.

Holly noticed her calm gaze and how carefully she listened to the bedtime instructions. The sight of her little boy and Ashleigh sitting there at the kitchen table, their heads close together, filled Holly with a feeling of goodness. She had to try not to stare. She grabbed her bag and held her keys in one hand.

'I'll be back by 10.30 as I don't want your mum worrying!'

'It's my dad, actually,' Ashleigh replied without looking up from Stanley's felt-tip drawings.

'Oh, OK, well, have fun… Bye then!'

Holly pulled the front door closed behind her and walked along to the stairs, thinking I'm winning – look at me! It felt like a new beginning. Childcare's the key, the be all and end all. Especially for a single mum. Look at me now! She nearly danced on the stairs, pushed the lock release and headed, humming, out on to the street.

Singing made her feel supported, lifted up. Something about the mixture of all their different voices, blending, it had an effect on her. It was full of unmatching things that made perfection. She remembered her mum's button jar. As a kid she played with it for hours, turning it like a kaleidoscope. Plain ones, rolling around with sparkly ones, all different sizes, even some toggles. She used to shake them out and arrange them into families. It became something else when you leant back, squinting your eyes to get the glazed vision, the whole. And that's what singing felt like.

Maybe all the good things are made up of lots of small things, she thought, maybe it's life! I'm part of a connected world, we're all here together! When she remembered it later it was so perfect, that night, the singing, then the pub, everyone saying cheers – how good life was! That pint of lager was the taste of freedom – god, it was the taste of being young. That first ice-cold gulp, it felt like skiving off, like someone would catch her and go, 'Oi, get back where you belong!' The best kind of pint.

And what a night. The pub was rammed and the Olympics opening ceremony was on the big screens. They arrived at the exact same moment when everyone ran outside spilling their drinks because the Red Arrows were doing a flyover – right there across the skies of London, streaks of brilliant colour for all the people to see, every single person in this hard old city, all looking up and cheering! It was like footy but with no opposite team: everyone was winning. Everyone talked to complete strangers. Holly joked, I'm from Yorkshire and even I'm a Londoner tonight! It was the best night ever.

But then, oh god. Why did it have to be this night? Holly had hugged her singing group plus several strangers and rushed off, the happiness shining out of her, back for 10.30 on the dot. Ashleigh was packed and ready to go. Such a pro – quickly outlined their games, brushing teeth, everything a mum wants to hear. Holly thanked Ashleigh energetically, gave her a crisp £20 and off she went. Worth every penny, Holly thought. Those exact words.

Still glowing, Holly looked in on her sleeping boy and kissed his head. She sat down on the sofa with a pleased sigh. She might catch the rest of the ceremony on telly but for now she wanted to be in the moment and think about things. About her place in the world. About feeling like a Londoner for the first time – it doesn't matter where you came from, it's where you are now! Stan was a Londoner and she was proud. Proud of their lives and how good they were going to be. Maybe with a snack. Maybe a tinny. She went into the kitchen.

For ever afterwards it was this next bit that played through her head like a film. She went to the kitchen cupboard, opened it, and saw the tin behind the cereal. She didn't know why, but she picked it up and looked inside. And that's when she saw it. That's when she saw. Her heart went loose. All gone. Her money was gone. The six tenners, two fivers and the two pound coin. No loose change, because that was too easy to borrow out of. The full exact £72. More than half way to the £125 she was saving up for his bike. His Christmas bike. Stanley's Christmas bike.

Holly pressed her eyes with her hands and swayed, a wave of sick came up in her belly. She'd put a fiver in just last week. But the tin was empty. She shook it, pointlessly, stupidly. There were a few crumbs stuck in the crack, like an insult. She must have stared at the inside of that tin for about a minute, breathing faster and faster. Then she walked back to the sofa, stood still, breathed twice more and picked up her phone.

She looked at it then put it back down again and collapsed on to the sofa. All of her bounce, all her joy in the world was gone. She was trying to hold the shock down. In front of her was the small table, her phone lying there. She sat, fingers interlaced, staring at it. She picked it up again, turned it round then put it back again, face down. The sick was bubbling up. All those courses in child protection and she'd gone and left her own baby with… with – who the hell even was this Ashleigh person?

What should she do? Should she call the other mums? They were all on the Year Two parent list. But those mums wouldn't give her the time of day. She unhooked her bra and wriggled out, pulled it out the side of her T-shirt and threw it on the floor. She rubbed her hands together and placed them over her eyes, feeling the warmth soak in. She massaged her scalp, urging her head to think of a way. She flopped back, and shifted to pull a Lego brick out from underneath her bum.

I can fix this, she thought, it's like part of my job. It's how you manage the badness. It's the same when you're a mum, anyone can do the easy stuff. Anyone can have a laugh and draw pictures and sing 'Wind the Bobbin Up' and wash his hair and make pancakes. It's the hard stuff that counts. It's the stuff that rips your insides. It's torment, thinking, Did I do it right? Was it too much? You feel sick about it. Then you go and look at him, asleep, arms flung open like perfect trust, and you want to cry, and you just want to love him more, make him safe in the world, and it hurts…

No one can share that, you can't know it until you do it. She would never complain about being a mum. Never. Although sometimes it could almost crush her, it wasn't a burden it was something else. It was heavy but it was the opposite of a burden. It was like, it was like the weight of real love. She had a sharp pure feeling in her chest. The feeling that came whenever she counted up the time that she didn't spend with him, how much she missed, how it never came back. What was it her mum had said in the early days – don't ever wish it away.

Holly stood up and pulled off the blanket that covered the worn-out patch of the sofa. Two more bits of Lego flew out from its folds. She spread it smooth again and sat down. Most kids nick stuff, she thought, trying to be reasonable. Ashleigh is still a child. Was Ashleigh OK? Children were everyone's job. Work had taught her this. She had started telling off teenagers for dropping litter. She covered her eyes again.

At what point did her job cross over into caring about other kids too? What was the quote on the wall at work: It's easier to build strong children than repair broken men. The thought of broken men led to Stanley's dad and the failure of all her hopes. Her mum said it was her fault for always trying to fix people. But if there were things you couldn't fix – did that mean you should never try? The trick must be to expand out from what she felt for Stanley. Start with who you love, she thought, and expand it from there.

But – but stealing the money for his Christmas bike! She sat up straight and picked up her phone. One more time. She dialled Ashleigh's number and it went to voicemail. She hung up and ground her teeth. Then she called again. As it rang she cleared her throat and this time she left a message: 'Ashleigh, it's me, Holly. I know what you've done. You need help. Call me back and tell me that you've done it and that you need help. If you don't do this I will have to call the police.'

She hung up and leant back heavily, gripping her arms folded over her chest. She rolled her head from side to side, heavy, her whole body was weighed down. The flat was silent.

27

SAMINA STOPS

'Samina? Samina, my darling, I will leave it here for you.'

Her dad bent slowly down and placed the tray on the floor outside her bedroom. He adjusted it so it was parallel to the door. He had placed a cup of sweet tea next to the plate of lamb tashreeb. He had folded a tissue beneath the knife and fork, then taken it out, because it was ridiculous to pretend to be a restaurant, but then he put it back again, because what if it made her smile? Food on a tray – he looked at it as he straightened his back – like food in a prison. He sent the thought away. He knocked gently on her door, paused and moved away.

This wasn't something he had ever had to do in his life before. He cooked for his children, yes, and cared for them when they were sick, of course. He tried to guide them always in the best way he could. But this was something new. She was a woman now. What was needed? Should he use softness or strength, how should he talk to her? He had never seen her this way. He had never seen his daughter give up.

When the police came to their flat and announced they were issuing a harassment warning, Samina first laughed and then she argued with them. They told her to sign a paper – it doesn't mean you're guilty, they said, but you should sign to show you've received it:

A complaint has been received and a charge may follow if the harassment complained of is repeated.

That was when he said to her – Samina, do as they say! Because what father can see his child disobey the police, and as a foreigner too? So she signed the paper and they went away. But that wasn't the end of it. Hadn't he warned her that things could flow in both directions? Could there be a more bitter curse, than for your warning to your child to come true?

Then her university tutor confirmed that these warnings remain on police files indefinitely, and that they can be disclosed later. This placed her studies in law in jeopardy. And that was the final blow. It took him back to the old days in Baghdad. The Old Man did things thoroughly. If you got reported then that was the end for you and for your whole family too. He had seen this, many times. But he thought it was different here.

He walked stiffly back into the kitchen area and stood still for a moment, wiping his eyes. Mal was on the sofa spreading out in all directions. At the sight of his father he sat up and tidied himself into a more acceptable shape.

'Is she… did she say anything?'

'No.'

'I still think we should go and visit that woman, sort her out, or spread some lies about her and see how she likes it.'

'That will not solve anything. The best revenge is to live well.'

'Yeah, that's great, Dad, but I'm saying – she can't stay in there for ever.' Mal sounded whiny, childlike. 'Dad, you have to tell her.'

'The plan for tomorrow belongs to tomorrow.' His voice was flat, he stood there, still facing away, in the middle of the kitchen floor.

'Dad.'

But there was no response. Mal frowned and leant forward, propping his elbows on his folded knees and rubbing the muscles in his neck. Typical, he thought, wheeling out the old proverbs when he couldn't think of anything else to say. What use was that? Their mum wouldn't have stood for it. She would've done something. Someone had to pull Samina out of this. He stretched his arms, cracked his knuckles and stood up. He went to her room, knocked on the door and then without waiting knocked again, harder.

'Samina, I know you're stronger than this.' He heard his own voice and tried not to sound like begging. 'You can't stay in there. You can't give up. If you don't come out…'

He leant his head on the doorframe and looked down at his feet in his white towelling socks. She'd always been the one to push him, to support and encourage and nag him. It was always her. It drove him mental, but now… Couldn't he just say it, we need you? He ran his thumbnail along the edge of the doorframe where the gloss paintwork met the wall. He looked back down at the food, untouched on the tray next to his feet. He took a breath and addressed the shiny paint of her closed door.

'Mum used to say that thing about power. What is it… The power we have is greater than we know.'

Mal's voice constricted. He gulped. He moved his weight from foot to foot and bunched his fists. Power, he thought bitterly, he'd never had less. Being sacked from Milwards hadn't bothered him that much. He could get another job easy. But his sister had properly tanked. It knocked her down and it was like she couldn't get back up. He'd always wished that she'd fuck up, just a bit – just to give him a break. But now it was happening he hated it. It scared him. He hoped his dad wasn't listening. He dropped his voice and spoke to the crack of the door.

'OK, listen, if you don't come out I'm going to take this food of yours and eat it. On the sofa. And I'm staying there all week, watching daytime TV – no CV, and no job applications.'

He paused.

'It's on you.'

It was a phrase he'd heard her use. He paused again then leant back into the door, his face right up to the crack.

'On the sofa. All day. Watching *Countdown. Home and Away. Loose Women...*' he whispered. 'Full volume, man, eating wings and daytime TV, I swear!'

He waited, straining his ears for any response from inside.

'*Cash in the Attic*, innit. *Deal or No Deal*, all day long...'

He heard a movement on the other side of the door and quickly backed away. The handle turned and the door gradually opened up a few inches. Samina looked out from the space between the frame and the door's edge. He caught his breath and held it in. Her face looked swollen and sort of squashed, there were crusty bits round her eyes and her hair was messed up. He stepped back further. The room behind her was dark. She looked bad. He struggled to keep his face neutral, not daring to show fear or humour or anything at all. She looked down at the food on the tray then slowly back up at him.

'Don't say "innit".' She gave a weary smile. 'You little bastard.'

He smiled too, and tears came into his eyes.

28

HOLLY IS LATE

'Don't forget your pens!' Holly was trying to get Stanley into his shoes and out the door. They were both knackered – it was nearly seven o'clock. 'Get a shuffle on! We're already late.'

They hurried down the corridor, past the shouty flats, the friendly ones, through all the different noises and cooking smells. Tonight was the annual meeting of the Tenants and Residents Association. She had to show up for the tenants because the lease-holders were so much better organised. Maureen always said, 'They look down on us, acting like they own the place.'

'Yeah, because they do!' Holly would reply and they'd laugh.

The whole weekend she'd had this plunging seasick feeling inside about Ashleigh. She'd called three more times but not left another message. The missing money made her guts turn over every time she thought of it, but it was more than that. It was the thought that there must be something wrong with Ashleigh, that there was a problem she could fix.

Stanley was whining about not having his glitter glue, asking could he go back because you can't do dragon wings with a normal pen. She ignored him as they took to the stairs. But what should she do next? Was it enough just to get her own money back? Could she do better, find out what was happening, try to make things OK again? It's kind of my job, she thought – OK, maybe not my official job title, but still, it's what I do. Take on a problem and fix it. But not this.

They reached the bottom of the stairway and Stanley pulled back on her hand, shouting 'No, Mummy!' and Holly bumped herself out of her thoughts. She'd forgotten, they always jumped the last three steps in one. They ran back up together and she jumped down with him, laughing as they hit the lock release button and ran outside.

Two elderly dogs were sitting tied to the bike racks near the hall door. They wagged and stood up to greet Stanley, but Holly steered him straight ahead and in through the door, mouthing a 'Sorry!' to the group. The first words she heard were 'certain tenants' and she knew the same old people were complaining about the same anti-social behaviours. Saba and Maureen were at the back pulling out extra seats, and on the side were tables set with tea, coffee and biscuits.

Stan sat on the floor with Saba's girls and they started colouring in his book. Holly crept to the back, sat down into a moulded plastic seat and let her bag slide on to the floor. The secretary was listing actions from the meeting with the construction consultancy group doing the council's building works. There was a ripple of grumbling noises whenever the word 'delay' came up.

A man sitting at the front asked about 'decanting' and whether it meant more flats would be sold. The chair suggested he find out more by joining the finance sub-committee. Nice shutdown, thought Holly. Next up, fly-tipping and security doors. The woman sitting next to her tutted. Her security door maintenance had been outsourced, she whispered to Holly with an eyeroll. 'Same with the fire alarms, meeting after meeting. What's the point!'

Holly gave a sympathetic nod. The woman looked familiar. Holly leant over and asked, 'Have you got kids at Avenue Road?'

'No, mine are older, they go Selby High. I'm Sian.'

'Hi, I'm Holly.'

Selby High, Holly thought, that's where Ashleigh goes. 'You don't know Ashleigh, do you, lives over on Tanghall?'

Sian's expression hardened and Holly felt the temperature drop. She continued, faltering, 'Well, it's… actually, do you know her dad? I was hoping to get his number.'

Sian pursed her mouth and took a breath. 'Yes. Why?'

'I just…' Holly felt her cheeks flush. Did Sian think she was trying to wangle a date? That had been a long time! 'How do you… how do you know them?'

'I knew her mum,' Sian said, speaking quietly. 'A long time ago. Ludi, I knew him, later…'

Holly was confused. 'Later…?' she echoed. Did that mean they'd talk later? Sian slowly shifted her unblinking stare away. Holly sat. What the hell just happened? They both looked ahead at the chair of the TRA, who was wearily working through the Any Other Business section that always got hijacked by the guy who complained about resources being spent on tea and biscuits. While eating a biscuit.

She sneaked a sideways look at Sian. This was the first person she could talk to who knew something about Ashleigh's family. But by her reaction, it wasn't good. As the meeting ended and people began to stand up and chatter, Holly put on her professional smile and turned to face Sian again.

'Listen, can we have a quick cuppa? Do you have time?'

They went over to the tea table. In the queue Holly got straight to it. 'Ashleigh stole from me and I'm worried about how much trouble she's in.'

Sian poured hot water into two plastic cups.

Holly continued in a hushed voice that she thought the dad didn't know but that he should be told.

Sian removed the teabags and put milk in both cups without asking. Then she looked up and stared at Holly again. 'Didn't she get referred to your lot though?'

'What!' said Holly.

'Well you should know – you're welfare, aren't you?'

'What? No! I mean – I'm only admin, I just do the… you know…' Holly shuffled the biscuit tray. 'Why do custard creams always come in threes!'

Another one who hates social workers, then. Holly tore open the clear biscuit packaging as her mind raced ahead – was Sian saying Ashleigh had been on the child-protection register? Sian walked off, carrying both cups of tea. Holly followed. The last thing she wanted was to report Ashleigh. She knew her team was drowning in high-risk cases, long-term vulnerable, unaccompanied refugee children, you name it. At best Ashleigh would be a juvenile justice case and get handed over to the police.

They sat down and Sian began to speak. 'I knew them, back in the day. Ludi got reported, a while after the whole Diane thing. After she'd gone. The neighbours heard screaming and that. He was sent to the GP, depression. I tried to warn him. He wasn't coping,' Sian looked down at her tea. 'He's got a heart of gold but I couldn't be around it any more.' She pushed back her braids, visibly closing that thought down. 'Anyway.'

She lifted her cup and took a long deliberate sip as if to say, That's that. Holly's mind was jumping. She felt an odd pang of loyalty to this dad, trying to cope on his own. She could see that Sian wanted this to be over. But she still needed more.

'Ashleigh seems very bright. She was so nice, I just can't understand.' Holly wriggled slightly. 'She babysits for the other mums too.'

'Yeah.'

Sian had put her cup down and was glaring straight ahead, arms folded over her chest. Anyone looking from across the hall would have thought it was a disagreement about whose turn it was to stack chairs.

'So can you share her dad's number? Was it, Ludi?' Holly asked. Sian waited a bit longer before she shrugged and got her phone out. She began to scroll through the contacts, eyes down, then held her phone out. 'Here. If it's still his number.'

'Thanks. I'll talk to him,' Holly carried on, 'to Ludi. And Ashleigh. To both of them.' She put her phone away and looked down at her tea.

'So,' Sian put her phone away too. 'Ashleigh babysat for you. So you know about her mum? And all that?'

Holly nodded uncertainly.

'You know everyone thinks she's dead?'

'What?'

Sian regarded Holly with a joyless half-smile. 'You lot, you don't know as much as you think, do you?'

29

TARA DOESN'T COME

'Mummy!'

Tara moaned against the whining sound, the rush of incoming wakefulness, the arrival of noise and light. She rolled over on to her front, pulling the duvet over, and buried her face in the crook of her arm. She was pushing, grinding her hips into the mattress to keep that feeling going. It was that dream. She felt like a teenager, throbbing with hormones, aching down deep. The ache moved up inside her thighs. Her full bladder added to the pressure. It was the sex dream. It was him, again. She kept her eyes shut, heart racing, body glowing.

'Mummy!'

No. She wanted to stay asleep, to stay with him in the dream, there, arching her lower spine like a cat, moving only so slightly, slightly, his hand on the back of her neck, holding just a bit too tight, his other hand peeling down the Lycra off her skin, touching her burning back. She held her breath. Like this? You like this? Yes. She sighed and closed her eyes tighter, moved her legs apart, oh god, yes, his chest, her hands inside his T-shirt, sliding down...

'MUMMY!'

'For god's sake, Tara!'

Giles pulled the duvet sharply back over to his side, shaking the bedframe as he sat up and swung his feet out of bed.

161

'So you're just going to ignore her?'

He went and yanked the curtains open, moving them back with a loud sweep. She tried to close her face, quickly turning away, but the sunlight came flooding in like a trumpet blast.

'Daddy's coming, Betsy.' He stomped back across the room and she could hear the sound of him scratching his armpit and sniffing.

'And I still haven't found those dollars,' he grumbled. 'As if I don't have enough other shit going on at work.'

Tara's breath came out slowly like an invisible puncture. Her eyelids twitched and parted dully. Mummy's not coming.

'You forgot to get bog roll again,' he shouted back over his shoulder as the bedroom door slammed.

30

HOLLY GOES

Holly took the morning off. She couldn't figure out any other way. Stan had to be at the holiday club, so daytime was the only option. Once she'd dropped him off she waited a while looking at Ludi's number. It rang long enough for her to hope for voicemail so she could hang up.

But he answered. 'Hello?'

She said she knew Ashleigh from school and needed to visit, to see them.

He paused. 'What? What's wrong?'

She said it was better face to face and she could get there in ten minutes.

She'd heard of Tanghall Estate but never been in before. It was three tower blocks overlooking a square with a sign saying No Ball Games. She found the right block; the main door was jammed open, so she didn't buzz but took the stairs up. Only two flights to go. She got her breath back as she counted along the corridor and – there. She knocked on the door, and again found herself wishing that no one would answer.

It opened and a man looked out. He had a pale, determined face and light brown eyes, he was younger than she expected, and attractive if he wasn't so tense, so guarded-looking.

'Ludi?'

He gave her a look like it was only a matter of time before everything went wrong. Then he said, 'Come in. Tea's on.' He left the door wide open, went through to the kitchen area at the back and took two mugs out of the cupboard. Holly stepped inside and looked around. She was in a small living-room area, between the sofa and the telly. It looked like there was only one bedroom. She pulled the door shut behind her and stood there. Ludi rattled around in a drawer then put a teaspoon on the side.

'Nice view,' Holly said in the general direction of the balcony at the back. It was warm and the air was thick with no-eye-contact tension. A pigeon landed then flew straight off again from the balcony wall. There was folded-up bedding next to the sofa and laundry on all the radiators. Holly didn't know any single dads, not even through her work. She'd never really thought of the possibility of one before. On the shelf was a row of school photos, two girls' startled smiles in cardboard frames.

'Ah, you've got a younger one!'

'Morgan's on a sleepover,' Ludi said. He was standing by the kettle, staring at it as though it might disagree with him.

OK, so much for the small talk. Holly smoothed back her hair and cleared her throat. She asked Ludi whether Ashleigh had told him anything, whether he knew what this was all about.

He moved the mugs around on the side and didn't look at her.

She carried on. 'I'm sorry to say this, but Ashleigh stole from me. She stole my money when she was babysitting for me the other night.'

Ludi didn't react, his fingers stayed on the mugs. She told Ludi it would probably be best to try to listen first and not

164

get upset. She added that there might be a way to find help. 'We should talk to her,' she said. 'I want to help. I know she babysits for other Year Two mums too – Stacey, Charlotte, Tara – but I don't know if she's… you know… if they've…'

Holly trailed off. Ludi didn't say anything.

'Obviously Ashleigh's still a child,' she went on, 'but I will need the money back.'

She paused. He was still staring at the mugs. What was wrong with him? What did she think was going to happen when she marched in here? She raised her eyes to the ceiling in frustration then looked back to Ludi. Finally he looked up.

'Who are you?' he demanded. 'Are you welfare?'

The kettle boiled and switched itself off. 'I'm just here as a mum,' she said quietly. 'I'm a parent too, Ludi. Doing my best, on my own – I know how that feels.'

In a lower voice Ludi said he didn't know anything, but that Ashleigh wasn't herself lately; he wasn't sure. He looked down again.

'Where is she?'

He paused. 'I'll try and call her.' He got his phone out and dialled. Holly didn't want to be listening in, but it wasn't easy in a place this small so she pulled out her phone out too and stared at it.

'No answer,' he said. 'But I think I know where she is.'

'Right?'

'She goes to an old neighbour's place – she has a study room in his garage. It's her…' He swallowed. 'She calls it her homework club.'

'Shall we go?'

He shrugged, then pushed the mugs away and gestured to the door. They went all the way down, and out of the estate. They didn't talk. They went past where the big trees were, where she and Stan got conkers in the autumn. Ordinary old London was all around them. They turned a corner and walked past hedges and front gardens. They walked wrongly together like two strangers who were accidentally side-by-side. Holly tried to catch his eye but he was looking ahead and his mouth was locked tight.

Suddenly he paused in front of an overgrown front garden and quietly spoke. 'Nicky's house.'

Holly looked up. 'I know the next-door one – it's Tara's house! I had to drop her cake tin back after the fair last year, but she wasn't in. It is this one, isn't it?'

But Ludi's face was turned away. Slightly set back and in between the houses was a garage space that looked like it had been made into a shed or workshop. They went up to the door. Ludi put his hands in his pockets.

'This is where she…' he stopped.

'Shall I?' Holly reached out and knocked.

Nothing. She looked round to the right at the front door of the house. It didn't look like anyone was in. She looked back at the garage door and knocked again, firmly. Then, Sod it, she thought, and tried the door.

As it opened there was a rush from inside, a scurrying noise and a cry of '*NO!*'

Ashleigh rushed towards them, trying to fill the doorway and block them out.

Holly stepped back. 'Ashleigh? We need to talk to you.'

'You can't be here!' Ashleigh's eyes were frantic, face blotchy, scalp red. Her voice went higher. 'Go away!'

Ludi stepped forward. 'Ash let us in.'

'Wait! No!' her voice was anguished. Holly stood aside in clumsy horror as Ludi moved forwards, crowding his daughter back inside through the garage door. He followed her in.

Holly floundered behind them in the doorway, as the father and daughter stood glaring at each other.

'What you doing…?'

'Get off me! Don't fucking touch me!' Ashleigh's voice was a quiet strangled scream as she lunged at Ludi and pushed him in the chest. Her hair was wild, she was blazing. She caught sight of Holly hovering behind Ludi and hissed 'You! It was you!'

'Ashleigh, we want to help!' Holly heard herself speak but felt helpless, appalled by the transformation before her eyes. Ashleigh pushed her hands up into her hair and rubbed, making a groaning noise like a trapped animal. She covered her face and sank down to squat on the ground.

In the pause that followed Ludi backed away a step. He looked like he was trying to shrink. Holly didn't move. No one said anything, and they were standing there, a triangle of misery in this garage space.

'Ashleigh,' Ludi said, looking around them now, his eyes widening as he looked, 'Ashleigh, what's happening here?'

Holly looked down at the girl, folded small on the floor. She was muttering; they could hear her breathing loud and rough, then suddenly she surged back up. Ashleigh stood up tall right in front of them. She ignored Holly completely, and looked Ludi directly in the face. She had turned from that electric devil-person all the way back into a girl. A pale girl in a rainbow T-shirt and falling-down socks. Her eyes were steady now; her face didn't tell anything at all.

'Ash?' he repeated, less certainly.

Holly was full of vivid fear, pity, disgust, she couldn't tell which. Ashleigh didn't blink her grey eyes. Watching her was like seeing a trapped animal. A chemical soup turning into something else. Holly was mesmerised.

167

Ludi seemed to be frozen now. Was he scared of her? His breathing made a noise but he didn't say any more. Holly wished he would speak, say something, anything. What should she say? What the hell was this place? She looked back at Ashleigh.

'Dad.'

Holly would never forget what Ashleigh said next – it made her whole back go cold.

'Dad. If you call the police you will never see me again.'

She said it flat – there was nothing inside her voice. And she raised her chin just a little bit, and she walked out the door.

31

SAMINA COMES BACK

Samina and Mal were flopped on the sofa together. She looked like she'd been asleep for a year, she was tousled and her eyes looked bruised. But at least she was out of her bedroom. Mal and his dad had exchanged a hopeful glance when they saw her back to her usual ways of writing away at the kitchen table with a pile of books around her. Now she was here with him, watching TV together, just channel-surfing, and every so often Mal looked sideways at her. She was wrapped up in a huge dressing gown over her fluffy pyjamas and slippers. She pushed both her feet up against his leg and shunted him along.

'Move yourself, you lump!'

'Listen, girl,' Mal elbowed her back, 'you're in my world now – you better learn to respect the rules of my office life!'

He reached over her to snatch the TV remote and the bowl of crisps from her side of the sofa. She trampled his leg again with her feet and laughed. He flicked through the channels, singing along to adverts as they sat for a while, munching away. When Mal spoke again, his voice sounded extra casual. 'So did you mean all that about never going back?' He turned the remote over and fiddled with the battery panel on the back. 'We can't both specialise in college dropout. Find your own way, don't copy mine.'

'Oh, don't worry, I'm planning my next moves,' Samina smiled lazily and ate a crisp.

'Shank her! Kill her family?'

'No!' She held another crisp between her finger and thumb, rolling her eyes at him. 'I'm not interested in revenge and neither should you be.'

'So is it I get sacked and I'm the same old, you get sacked and suddenly you have the wisdom of Yoda?'

Samina rotated the crisp in the air and spoke in a Jedi voice: 'To live well, the best revenge is!'

Mal was so light with relief he couldn't take the smile off his face. Her disappearance behind that bedroom door had almost paralysed him. They had been left waiting, hanging there, and Dad had done nothing; creeping around with his trays of food, for all his wisdom he had no idea. But now Mal felt the deepest fears were draining out of him, he could feel it in his limbs. He had got his family back. He stretched out his legs, reached his hands over his head and cracked his knuckles.

'OK, I can't wait so let me guess: forgive everything and move on – am I right?' He cocked his head to the side and went on, counting the options on his fingers: 'Be the change you want to see in the world, be Daddy's favourite golden girl, become even more holy than you was before?'

'You are such a dick.' She stacked five crisps into a heap and pushed them all into her wide-open mouth at once, chewed thoughtfully a few times then stuck her tongue out at him like they used to.

'What, then?'

She swallowed the crisps and cleared her throat. 'I can challenge the police warning and clear my name. What happened to me,' she licked salt from her fingertips, 'was a de facto verdict without trial.'

CHAPTER 31

'Talking in Latin – that'll show the feds.'

She ignored him. 'Otherwise what's the point of studying law? I could be a test case. I've prepared my deposition on the inequitable consequences of the warning—'

'Yes!' he high-fived her.

'I'm not joking! It's ready, and I'm going to start by taking a copy over to Tara's house.'

'Boom!' He shot a gun with his fingertips. 'And she is gonna love that.' Mal leant back and raised his eyebrows at her, trying not to act too impressed. She was definitely back – this was his sister.

'Also,' she went on, 'maybe I got off lightly, you know, with Tara? I don't think even she knows the impact she has.' She ate another crisp. 'That woman is a crime wave. After what happened with their old cleaner, I never met the new one, but there was a babysitter too – I met her once at school pick-up.'

'Yeah?'

'Ashleigh. She's still at school – she's just a kid,' Samina sat up, frowning. 'I wonder if I should maybe warn her.'

'Strong is the Force with this one,' Mal whispered cinematically.

'And you,' she turned and looked at him. 'What about you, then, little brother?'

'I told you.' He grinned. He threw a crisp up in the air, failed to catch it in his mouth, picked it off the front of his T-shirt and ate it triumphantly. 'This is my office right here. De facto. You're trespassing, innit.'

171

32

HOLLY SEES

A long, crushing moment passed when Ashleigh walked out the door. Holly looked at the space where Ashleigh had been, and at her own hands and shoes, but not at Ludi. Near them some old tools hung from a row of hooks by the garage door, and opposite on the back wall was a window on to the garden with a desk below. Holly stared. The further into the space, the less normal it looked. The first thing was a face on the wall. A large black-and-white photocopy of a photo of a woman, you could tell it was old by the clothes and hair. She stared defiantly out like What are you looking at? Long hair, and the same big eyes. It had to be Ashleigh's mother.

'She's mental,' Ludi whispered. 'She's like her mother.' He was standing facing away from Holly and she could see his neck, and his back moving slightly with his breathing.

She didn't answer; she took a step further in. Across the back of the garage wall on either side of the desk were stacks of boxes and bags. Small glossy paper bags with satin ribbon handles. Shiny cardboard boxes. Bigger cardboard bags, embossed. They looked new and unopened. The back wall and both sides were covered in a display of papers and items spreading down on to the floor and outwards in repeating circular patterns and shapes, papers, pages, business cards and letters.

'It's like… a gallery?' Holly spoke slowly. 'Ludi?'

He didn't answer. She moved over to the side of the room, up to the wall, and her hands were clamped. Ashleigh had created a whole, god knows what, a secret world of her own in here. There was all sorts. Letters and lists and memos and Post-it stickers. All in different handwriting. Post! She was taking people's post? Pages, stuff, writing – and all lovingly arranged and displayed; it looked like an organised system – what was it? It was curious, almost beautiful. And it went on and on. Holly turned her head from side to side as she scanned up and down.

Wait – look! 'Stanley!' Holly burst the silence. There on the wall was a sheet of Stanley's maths exercises, and in the middle of the page on top of a triangle was stuck a small photo that she'd last seen on her own kitchen pinboard. Right there staring off the page on the wall, from her own home – it was her and Stan in the photo booth at Morrisons. The top of his head and one eye, and her laughing. With a narrow white border. There in the middle of the wall of fame.

Holly touched it with her fingertips then moved on, along the creepy exhibition, looking, with no idea what she was seeing. Whatever it was, she didn't want Stanley to be in here. She glanced over at Ludi again; he seemed similarly stunned. They were both moving uncertainly along like tourists in a temple. She turned back, and her heart speeded up to find herself at the start of a winding trail of ten and twenty-dollar bills.

'How! How did people not notice all this was missing?' she asked out loud. Ludi said nothing. Maybe he hadn't seen the money yet. The dollar bills were placed end to end, pale green and narrow, and then curled into a fan shape around a half eggshell. It was broken cleanly and lay facing up, shiny inside. It looked like a normal eggshell, but to Holly it felt like in this place it might contain something awful. She reached down to touch it then drew her hand back, thinking, Oh god, this is so much worse than I thought.

Streams of scraps and bits and shreds, along and along. Receipts, business cards, National Theatre tickets, a torn sheet of scrap paper:

Ashleigh – He can have Calpol at 10 if he's still awake. Thanks ☺

A child's birthday party invitation

A family membership card for Kew Gardens

H&T Pawnbrokers Loans Against Your Jewellery

The business cards ran in a line along the edge of the floor, Holly bent down and picked one up.

Joao Milanes – crazy hot fitness.

She smiled. Lots of the posh mums had personal trainers – you'd see them in the park in their gleaming activewear, suffering away with some buff guy dominating them. She turned the card over and started – there on the back, in small simple hand-writing:

I want you so bad – lets do it again, my place?

Holly stared.

A few steps further along was the back of the room. She touched the handle of the top drawer of the desk and drew it open. Maybe her own money would be in here. She pushed a few pens aside and drew out a small old-fashioned pill box.

Oh no – jewellery? It rattled as she held it up. She opened it and inside was a wizened brown thing, a miniature shrivelled apple. She let it fall out on to the palm of her hand and looked closely. It was brown and leathery, almost weightless, dried out like a raisin-apple. She shook her head.

A groceries shopping list with a doodle of a face emerging from a tree

Europe SOS: a refugee leaflet from Amnesty International

A letter in blue crayon:

I LovE you Ashlieh beecase you our nice to me always When will you com?

WONGA Takeaway Menu: Gourmet 2 Your Door – international cuisine on speed dial

B-BACK GOLD – Gold Diamond and Watch Experts Free Evaluation

'Ludi,' Holly kept her voice steady and pulled out her phone, 'I think we need to call the other people she babysits for. I know who they are. I think they should know.'

Ludi was at the back of the room, in the other corner, going through the shiny designer bags.

'It's like designer shoes, expensive trainers – how did she get all this? She doesn't even…' Ludi trailed off, a pristine Nike hanging off his hand. 'How the hell did she get the money for stuff like this?'

'Listen, we've got to tell the other parents.'

Ludi looked down at the other shiny bags and boxes piled up. 'Wait – I can't – why? Can't we wait, talk to her? She's in trouble...' He began to put the trainer back into its box then looked back up at Holly. 'Can't I – what can I do?'

'She told me who her others are – I got their numbers, their addresses and that, it's all on the Year Two parent list. Hold on, I'll forward it,' she said, tapping away at her phone.

'But can't we try and fix it,' Ludi began.

'We have to warn them,' she said, looking up. 'Ludi, this is not OK.' She gestured around the room.

'Let me just at least warn them.'

Holly looked down, frowning at her phone. She dialled Charlotte's number; it rang out. She felt Ludi's eyes on her as she dialled again, this time Stacey. It was engaged. She rang twice more and sighed in frustration. Finally she scrolled down, and rang Tara's number.

'Or maybe just leave it,' Ludi tried again. 'For now, just—'

And Tara picked up. Holly took a deep breath.

'Tara, it's Holly, from school. There's a problem with Ashleigh, the babysitter – she's been... she's... stolen some things.'

'Listen, I'm just back from a run and about to get in the shower.' Tara had the kind of telephone voice that everyone else could hear. 'Can this wait?'

'Uh,' Holly turned away from Ludi and lowered her voice, 'it's... it's pretty bad.'

'Well, if she was stealing from me she'll be sorry!' Tara's reply was clearly audible. 'She will pay for this!'

Holly glanced back at Ludi, who looked paralysed as these words about his daughter began to spread out from this terrible place.

'We're in Nicky's garage, next door to yours.'

'Nicky's?! Next door!'

Holly looked at Ludi again. He was standing staring at her; she mouthed the word *sorry*.

'Stay there,' Tara said. 'I'm on my way,' She hung up.

Ludi looked scared. 'I can't stay.' He backed away towards the door. 'I've got to go.'

'Where?'

He was already halfway out. 'I've got to help her.'

'Listen, just call me, if…' Holly realised he'd gone and she was talking to no one. She turned back to the walls of weirdness. It pulled her like a magnet – if only it wasn't so awful – but it was hypnotic: what did it all mean?

A BOSE remote control, a Daewoo remote control, a Digibox three-in-one remote control

A condom tied in a knot, the gob of liquid rolling inside.

A heap of small marshmallows arranged in a pyramid

A NatWest bank statement

A fountain pen

Holly squatted down to look more closely, drawn in, but afraid to touch the display.

Clarins samples: purifying gel, hydrating cream

A thin lock of light brown hair, clipped together in a child's hairgrip with a cherry motif

£980.00 receipt from the Khan Centre for Reproductive Medicine

Prestige Pawnbrokers: Instant Cash

A hand-written note that had been screwed up and was now carefully unscrewed:

Giles I won't ask again. I can't take any more. STOP doing this. PS check your annual leave again I don't think they've got it right.

'What the actual fuck!'

Holly flinched at the sound of Tara's voice announcing its way in through the open garage door. She quickly moved away from the wall.

'Have you found any dollars?' Tara came in loudly. Her face was flushed, her hair was pulled back and she was still in her running gear. She had her phone in her hand. She stopped. 'What the hell *is* this?'

Holly gave a helpless shrug and looked around. 'She stole from me and you, and I think from Stacey and Charlotte.' In her rush to let them know, she hadn't figured out how to describe this to the other mums.

'Wow.' Tara sounded almost impressed. 'So it was Ashleigh all along!' She bent down near the open doors and began to take in the display at her feet.

'To think I sacked Samina for this!' She read out some of the flyers, receipts and business cards that were artfully displayed.

Cash Converters – We Pay Instant Cash!

Hatton Garden Bespoke Jewellers

New Bond Street – The Place for Diamonds

'Diamonds?! Who *is* she?'

33

ASHLEIGH RUNS

A series of bright explosions seemed to puff up behind her eyes as Ashleigh ran. She ran from the place. Her place. She ran flat out, and at first she held her breath – for almost half a block she ran like this, but then there were bright black spots in her eyes and she couldn't. She sucked in, heaving gasps of breath, but didn't stop running. She ran onwards and ran until her legs hurt, a burning pain, until the pain took over and everything else was far behind. She felt the sound of her footsteps like a beat, her heartbeat, sounding in her head; she could hear her insides, her lungs, her blood. She ran and ran.

The gallery she had been building, creating, for so long. It was so good, her secret place. And now it was over – they were right there inside it. They had invaded her, ruined it – it was the end of her gallery. Her stupid dad. She hated him. The idea that he might catch her out. He had never done anything, never been anywhere – it was disgusting how stupid and slow he was. Just the thought of him made her speed up. And Holly – Ashleigh's face twisted – thinking she's like some saviour. Interfering bitch. She would still have her own place if it wasn't for Holly.

She ran on, her feet pounding, pushing herself onwards. She could hear her own breathing, and she thought about her body moving from aerobic to anaerobic respiration. Her bones and muscles were like a machine. Then the pain came again, this time a stabbing feeling in her side. She slowed her running down, landing heavily as she lost momentum, each pounding footfall shaking her face, her bones. She stopped, coughed and doubled over. Lactic acid. Her calves and her guts were burning. She leant one arm on a wall and squatted down for a few moments to catch her breath and let her blood get to the right places. Then she breathed all the way in and stood right up, tall again, glowing. The anger made her strong. She went to move forwards again.

But her apple! She faltered. Her feet slowed and she hesitated in the middle of the pavement. The apple. She wobbled – she needed it. Her treasure. Where it all started. Should she go back? She turned and looked back along the road she'd just run down. She put her hand on a streetlamp. She knew they were still in there, inside her gallery – she could feel that they were there. What if they took it? She twisted, sharply, as if in pain. But she couldn't go back. She couldn't.

There was a building-up, a rising feeling in her guts and she knew if it got to her chest and upwards then it would mean she would have to start crying. She could not allow that to happen, and she could not go back. She blocked out the thoughts. She would keep moving. The city didn't know or care. She could go into it, vanish into it. She started again, moving her legs, powering her feet. I don't care about the stuff. Not about the stuff, she repeated inside her head. *It's not about the stuff,* the narrator voice echoed. *She's not down yet.*

Keep running. She was sweating and her hair was flying all over the place, and the road carried on in front and behind her. They were in her gallery, and maybe they'd even got the apple, but they still didn't know everything. No one did. That was what mattered. Her power was that no one knew all of it. So she still had control. Her jaw ached. She was running again.

CHAPTER 33

There were lots of places she could go. Her steps were eating up the pavement. She ran on and on and the pain began to fade. Down she ran, all the way down the traffic-jammed road and past the station. She still had her own life and she kept all the different parts of it separate. So no one knew all of them. It was all on purpose and exactly how she wanted it. Her running and her breathing got into their own rhythm.

I could've done it though, could've kept it! But Holly – that was the mistake. I shouldn't have taken from her. She ground her teeth in self-punishment, why did I do that, why? Holly's got nothing and that's why she noticed. Shit, shit. Ashleigh shook her head. Why did I do that? Why? Ashleigh repeated. All she knew was, she was right about people – they had to be kept away. No one could know her.

They would never understand. Her blood pumped and pumped away as she ran, she imagined its bright red movement. They'd probably think she was trying to be some kind of Robin Hood. Stealing from the rich to give to the poor? No. They had no idea. That was so basic. Ashleigh shook her head again. Where was the scope for imagination?

She bunched her fists as she sprinted to the other side of the road. A moped slowed and swerved round her then honked a rebuke as it passed, but she didn't even look. How about forget about the poor and infiltrate the rich, penetrate them, eat them from the inside. Like Darwin's wasp. Ashleigh's hair streaked behind her as she sped the long downwards stretch, she boosted her speed, her phone and keys bouncing in her pockets as her feet flew. *She can still win this.* Eat them, like a brilliant, deadly parasite.

34

TARA LOOKS

The pair of dark green silky knickers had a white lace trim. Tara recognised them. She reached out and picked them up, slowly unrolled them and looked inside. There was an almond-shaped thin white crust on the gusset. 'Oh god!' She recoiled and threw them back.

More photos, again and again that same repeating photo of the woman. Tara leant back to observe the face on the wall, that chin tilted upwards, the direct stare. 'So that's her mum, then,' she said. 'What happened to her, anyway?'

'I'm not sure.' Holly said from over on the other side. The women walked slowly and deliberately, pausing, crouching, looking and moving on. They sank into quietness. The only sound was an occasional deep exhalation. More pictures. There was another blown-up photo, also copied and enlarged; the pixelated faces of little Ashleigh and the baby sister in her arms.

A snow globe containing the Eiffel tower, an engraved cow bell on a red ribbon

A tiny pink sock

Doll's house furniture

A miniature piano

A small doll in a chair balanced on the back of a slightly larger doll lying face down

Gold Star Certificate: Lily-Mae Dubree was brave at the dentist today!

Receipts arranged in a fan shape

Hillgate School brochure: Where Your Child's Dreams Flourish

A plaster cast baby's footprint

Oxford University Charlotte Dubree BA Hons Certificate Third Class

'Ha!' Tara exclaimed. She knew Charlotte had gone to Oxford, never heard the end of it, but not that she got a crap degree. Tara's anger was supplemented by a juicy curiosity as her eyes scanned eagerly. What next?

Council-tax bills with addresses and tax-band categories marked out in orange highlighter

Certified Copy of an Entry of Death

A small tooth

EZ Money WHAT R U WAITING FOR Transform Your Stuff Into Spondoolas

A row of empty popped bubble strips – some kind of medicine?

'Oh god,' said Tara, looking closer at a sheet of headed hospital paper:

RE Patient discharge STACEY CROFT This patient is a 47 years old female who miscarried her pregnancy at gestation approx. 6-7 weeks. She had a procedure (D and C) to remove the contents of the uterus under GA which was straightforward/ without complications. She is otherwise fit and well with no significant medical history and no allergies. I have advised her to take simple analgesia and to return if her bleeding does not settle / she develops severe pain/pyrexia.

A series of flattened empty boxes framed the discharge letter, their labels facing upwards: Co-codamol, Paramol, Co-Dydramol, Tramadol, Codeine Phosphate, Dihydrocodeine

'Oh my god…' Tara leant closer. Stacey was some kind of junky?

Eight unmatched teaspoons, handles inwards, arranged pointing out in a flower shape

The same circular design made out of dried red rosebuds

Two keys

A tiny spiral of nail clippings, ranging upwards in size

A display of books, set out like a pavement library:

The Collected Poems of Thomas Hardy

The Geeks Shall Inherit the Earth: Popularity, Quirk Theory and Why Outsiders Thrive after High School

Crime and Punishment

A collage on Weetabix cardboard: painted pasta shells and glued string, sequins and glitter

A cartoon of a chicken wearing fake ears with a speech bubble saying Compare the Meerkat

ABRSM Grade 2 Violin Certificate: Orson Croft Grade: PASS

'Oh!'

Tara then found herself in the middle of an elaborate display dedicated to her husband. Stuck on to the wall with the writing side facing out was an old postcard from Spain, addressed to Giles. She looked quickly to see if Holly was looking then sank down and squatted on the floor to get closer. On the floor beneath the postcard was a printed series of screen-grabbed search histories:

Giles Birling, Giles Birling hot, Giles Birling wife, Twitter, Giles Birling hair, Giles Birling best story, Giles Birling net worth, Twitter, Northern Slags, Twitter, Dog Cum Good Boy, The Milk of Human Kindness, Twitter, Asian Babes, Girls-on-girls-on-girls, Twitter

She followed the trail of printed emails, carefully spread out in an overlapping curved display. She picked up the first page – it was dated last month.

Re: Formal enquiry
Dear Giles, further to the allegations of workplace harassment the victim wishes to allege racist abuse…

She went dizzy as her eyes skimmed ahead to the end. It was an exchange between her husband and his line manager. Giles' voice echoed in her mind: 'You need to get a job!'

She rustled the papers around dully as her head filled up and started to buzz inside. She turned them over and looked at their blank back sides as though there might be a hidden disclaimer somewhere. How on earth had Ashleigh got hold of these? Her mind was unable to keep up as she flickered backwards and forwards taking in random phrases and words: 'bullying enquiry'… 'discrimination'… 'political cor- ⁻rectness' and in capitals 'IS THIS BECAUSE I'M WHITE?'

Oh, Giles. Tara felt a loosening, spinning feeling, in her head, or maybe in her body, she put her hands on the ground to keep her balance. Her throat closed and she gulped repeat-edly. Her eyes blurred over as she shuffled the pages together into a heap. She twisted the crumpled pages in her hands. She would burn them. That girl… Her vision wobbled as she looked up to check whether Holly had witnessed this paper trail of her own private devastation.

Holly was over on the opposite side of the room near the back wall, a hand clasped over her open mouth. Tara stabi-lised herself with one hand on the wall and gradually got to her feet. It wasn't fair. It just wasn't fair.

'After the day I've had…' Tara said, still holding the gath-ered-up emails in her hands, the pages flapping as she wiped her cheeks. 'Someone has to call the police!'

'I hadn't realised how bad—' Holly spoke under her breath. 'But she's just a child!' Her voice was firmer now. 'We mustn't build up a kind of wall between us and that girl.'

'Well, I can't call them, not again!' Tara's voice was high-pitched. 'Twice in two months – they'll think I'm mad!'

They faced each other in a reluctant circuit of mistrust.

'Also,' Tara's face had gone a light grey colour. 'She knows about… she knows stuff. About us.'

35

LUDI GOES TO THE
FIFTH FLOOR

Ludi still couldn't feel that any of this was real, but he'd made his decision. He was going to fix it. He took the stairs, not the lift. After the first three floors he stopped and breathed quietly for a few moments in the stairwell. She still hadn't answered her phone, and he couldn't think of another way to do it. He hoped no one would see him.

He carried on up to the fifth floor and walked down the middle of the corridor. All the flats had the doors on the same side and balconies at the back, same as his. But he'd not been to the fifth floor for years. Never let his girls come up here, either. Even though they knew the kids in the end flat. He stood there and didn't knock on the door. He stood, and coughed.

How else was he supposed to make it OK? He looked both ways; there was no one else around. The next door flat had a welcome mat and a baby buggy outside the front door. Then the flat on the other side had a Union Jack and a Portugal flag hung inside a window covered in Olympics 2012 stickers. But this one here, just the same plain old front door, it hadn't changed at all.

Ludi coughed again, smaller this time, more of a throat-clear. It was how many years? Ages back, they'd tried to bring him in. Scabby Mark went on and on about coming to work for them, just try it out, doing lookout or deliveries: 'Neighbourhood watch, innit.' He'd said no. No way – never going to happen. And look at him now.

But up against the other bad stuff, this was nothing. Something's only bad until a worse thing comes along, and then you can't believe you're wishing for the old bad thing. He would swap any day. If only he could go back, he breathed. It wasn't about him any more, though; he didn't have a choice.

'If you call the police you will never see me again.'

Her words were like poison, like a burn or tattoo that would never heal over. Maybe he never knew her. With that cold stare of hers. Had he lost her too? Does anyone really know their own kids? Maybe it was his fault. Now she was gone, wouldn't answer the phone. Where was she?

Ludi gripped himself, told himself: I'm all she's got, we're here in the middle of this thing and I'm fixing it. That's what parents do isn't it. That's what we do. He ignored the bell and knocked hard on middle of the door, three times. He squared himself, legs apart, chin up, looking straight into the spy hole. He wasn't about to beg, that was for sure. Footsteps and a pause, and then the door open a crack.

Ludi stood straight and spoke gruffly. 'Yeah, I've changed my mind.'

Scabby Mark pulled the door all the way open, rested his arm up high on the doorframe and gave a little smile. Leaning there all greasy, all pleased with himself. Like he knew this would happen eventually, that Ludi would finally show up here again. Like it was nothing to be ashamed of. A warm smell floated out, the smell of ash trays and wet towels and skunk.

'What's that, then?' he said. 'You found Jesus?'

He was barefoot, and wearing shiny tracksuit bottoms and a vest with Homer Simpson as a Rasta. It was too tight. Ludi glanced away from the hairs in his white armpit.

'No, about the work.' Ludi cleared his throat. 'Doing stuff with… for you… you know.'

There – another smile. He was loving this. He wasn't as scabby as he used to be, Ludi noticed. But there was still something up with his eyelids, like they'd been barbecued. His hair was short and long, depending on the angle. His feet were babyish small, his toenails the same colour as tinned pineapple. Ludi kept his face blank.

'OK,' he said, and pushed himself off the doorframe, scratching his belly. 'You won't regret it. Easy money. Plus all the benefits of flexible working, ha ha! Step right in!'

He gestured past himself and back into the dark flat where the telly was blasting.

'Want a smoke?'

Ludi shook his head.

'Got a lot more young ones working now too – they're like under the radar – you know they can't get busted. I believe the children are our future!' he crooned, and chuckled to himself.

'Look, I need some money.'

'And that reminds me, how are those sweet little girls of yours?' Scabby Mark ploughed on, ignoring him. 'Not so little now,' he added.

The blood seemed to run out of Ludi's head and he couldn't speak. He swallowed the words that came: Don't mention my girls. Not here. He stayed put, looking through the door into the room. Clothes and dishes and tins were scattered around. He couldn't see the telly but he could hear the loud studio laughter. By the sofa there was a small lamp on the floor and a low table covered in gear. It was and always had been the last place on earth Ludi wanted to go.

'You still got the van?' Scabby Mark went on. 'We're doing more work out of town now and are always needing deliveries.'

The inside of that flat, the loudness, all the exact same, and that sticky smell seeping out. It was like a wave, a tide that pushed him back, moving against him. Stand straight! It was the smell though. Ludi felt it in his feet then his whole body, it brought everything back again. It was bad. He took a step back.

36

ASHLEIGH DOESN'T STOP

Ashleigh slowed down, changed direction and wandered some more. Away from the big roads were lots of small hidden roads with high layers of windows looking down, she was heading downtown. Down town. Torn down. Ashleigh hummed. Maybe this is where I'm supposed to be, she thought, dusty pavements, drains, drunken people broken teeth, old gates.

It was like she'd gone underwater and the sounds had all stopped. No one inside her head, nothing. She tried to stop the falling feeling, she strained herself against it, like struggling to get out of a dream. She reached deep into her mind for a good thing, and there wasn't one. Nothing was pushing her forward or away, she was just moving. All of the strange parts of the day, all of the noises in the world had merged into a kind of buzzing inside her, something she could feel but not hear.

The pavement widened out by the wall of an old church with huge gates. Behind them was a row of trees. Into the air beside her came a tiny cascade of noises, and she looked up, and there on the middle of a branch was a small bird. It was a plain dusty colour and its tail trembled as it sang. It was free to fly wherever and the sound was so pure that Ashleigh could almost taste it, she fell out of step. Behind it, the white clouds puffed and the sky was as blue as it had ever been.

Please, her mind whispered to the bird, please be on my side, and they were the first words to appear for a long time. As she carried on moving along Ashleigh felt like she was getting smaller and smaller and turning into a child. She wanted to run back and look for the bird, she wanted to turn and find it, a stinging started in her eyes. No.

She pinched her fingers together and they were there but with a kind of pins and needles feeling. She could just be leant against these railings here, balanced at the side of the road and left here like a cardboard hollow shell. Even the narrator voice wasn't there. The traffic, the tall gates, the bird, the pavement were all behind her now. What if she just went home and went to sleep? She moved and could not feel her limbs. She was so light. Was she a ghost?

She dredged around to remember the sense of herself. She had to anchor herself back into the world. She knew where to go. She was most of the way there already. She came round the back side of the building and through one of the side gates. Across the wide chessboard glamour of the court-yard, and in past the security guards on the heavy doors. This was how to block everything out. All the bad things. She was keeping them away, filling herself up with this instead, stopping them from disturbing her mind, from invading her, it was working.

'This one's not like the other libraries,' she said to herself. No, this one was a palace, a cathedral, it was Wembley. As always Ashleigh tipped her head back, taking in the space, the light, the stairways of the British Library. In the past Ashleigh had sidled up to the guided-tour groups, hitch-hiking along and admiring the 3D architect's plans with them. This time she ignored the pillar of golden books behind a glass wall.

She looked around and behind herself like an animal that can smell a predator, plunged into the half-lit glowing temple of the Treasures Gallery. In through its heavy doors like a top-secret vault. Ashleigh always thrilled to the world's first this, the world's first that, as though the treasures were her own. This was the inspiration for her own gallery. Collecting, displaying and understanding. Owning.

Her eyes adjusted to the green twilight. She went over to sacred texts, the golds and the blues, trying to soothe her mind. People are shit, she told herself, but the world isn't. She still had herself, her questions, her answers, her knowledge, herself. And at least it was dark in here. Glints of ancient gold shreds lit up from a nearby cabinet. She rubbed her sleeve hard over her eyes, refocused. Standing motionless, her eyes fixed on a many-armed Hindu god emerging from a fish next to a mountain spinning on the back of a turtle.

She stared, leaning her forehead into the glow reflecting from the manuscripts inside. Some of the books were suspended, open, like birds frozen in flight. Birds in flight. She looked up and felt the lower half of her face tremble. She was small and weak, and separated. She felt hunted. How, she thought, how do I get to not lose? She scanned the room, feeling like she too was locked away behind reinforced grey-green glass. What was the word in that poem? *Wistlessness.*

Where could she go? They were in her gallery. She couldn't go home. She couldn't go anywhere now. Ashleigh drooped, leaning on the wall, her hands fell loosely to her sides. Even here, the unchanged world came pushing its way back in, came after her. Her phone was buzzing in her pocket. She ignored it several times, shaking her head with the effort, and then, knowing it was wrong, she pulled it out and looked.

That was the mistake. She got a feeling like a net tightening around her heart.

The spell of the Treasures Gallery shrank away, and she slumped. Eleven missed calls and a stack of messages:

Call me!

Ashleigh call me back

I trusted you with Betsy and this is how you repay us?

WE KNOW ABOUT YOUR STEALING

Where are you?

Answer your phone

WHERE ARE YOU

Ashleigh's face hardened, her mouth set. She lowered the hand that was holding the phone. It was too late. The humiliation had hunted and caught up with her. She couldn't get away from this now, not even in her mind. She leant back against the wall again and clamped her eyes shut. It was over, then.

First they had gobbed and spat all over her privacy, her very own space, her own collection. And now here, like an oily tentacle, like leaking sewage, here inside the ultimate treasures, they polluted all this too. Ashleigh felt a rushing-up surge of injustice and it caught her in the chest.

'Trusted you with Betsy?' Ashleigh echoed. Betsy loves me more than that rancid cow. Tara wouldn't know treasure if it punched her in the tits. Tara didn't deserve Betsy. In her nasty red lipstick, her fake smiling, her shit husband, disgusting old bitch. She wished Tara was dead. Ashleigh pulled in a deep breath and looked up. The feeling came up from her chest and moved into her throat. Hot tears messed her vision.

Fuck Tara. Fuck her. Fuck all of them. Fuck their houses and their caring about genital mutilation and their sustainable coffee. Fuck their rounding up her pay with that little smile. Fuck their olive oil. Fuck their confidence, their big windows. Fuck their scruffy Converse and pretending to be poor. Fuck their arguments about equal pay and diversity. Fuck their precious children and all their children's violin tutors, maths tutors, scholarships. Fuck their yoga mats and their human rights. And fucking triple facefuck their endless winning, their guaranteed success.

They didn't know her. They did not know her. She could taste blood in her mouth. Her eyes blurred again and her mind blazed. She uncurled her fists as she left the Treasures Gallery. She walked through the entrance hall and back out of the building. Her nails left marks on her palms.

37

LUDI PAYS

Ludi stepped back on to the road and out into a different world. That was it – done. Four thousand pounds in tidy stacks of twenties. Did it show? Could people tell? Here, inside his jacket, envelopes inside another bigger envelope. He pressed the shape of it into his body, feeling the danger. It was thicker than he expected. It weighed, there was so much of it.

Should he call Ashleigh again? Maybe she'd answer this time. He wanted her to know it was going to be OK now, that she was safe from Tara and the others. He kept his eyes down and his heart from hoping. It rang out. He flexed his hands. He wasn't stupid, he knew how it worked – he was fucked. Scabby Mark was a clown but his people were serious. Now he was lost, so that Ashleigh didn't have to be.

It felt like the end of everything he'd put together in this life. In the time it takes to eat a packet of crisps. It was like that old game of Snakes and Ladders, which he always hated because of that long one back down. Real-life snakes. Tara, 'I'm going to make her pay!' And Scabby Mark, 'Welcome on board!'

Suddenly a buzzing, vibrating. He tore at his pockets and pulled the phone back out with a surge of panic. Was it – was it? Please god please god, please, let it be her. I'll do anything.

Turned it over with shaking hands to look at the screen. No. That nosy cow Holly again. Just leave me alone! He shoved it back in his pocket.

He walked onwards towards the high street. The Number 37 bus pulled past him with a sigh. He didn't look in case he saw anyone. Where did I go wrong? he asked himself. Did I work too hard, or not hard enough? And if their mum was here, would this still have happened? His mind just wouldn't stop.

Two pigeons landed in front of him and chased each other round. Some kind of sex dance. Mate, she's not interested. He almost laughed at it puffing itself up like that. He'd always liked pigeons, even if everyone hated them. They never felt sorry for themselves. You don't see a pigeon sat there depressed about having stumps for feet. They don't give up. Like being a parent – you can't give up. Whatever you might find out. That's just how it is.

He was proper losing it now – what the hell. Walking on and wishing he was a pigeon. So, their mother left them, him and the girls. Two calls from Aberdeen where she claimed to be a waitress, before the boyfriend on the rigs took her to Australia. And that was it. He'd gone into a spiral. Evenings were the worst. Watching Ashleigh and Morgan asleep at night, thinking, How can you take it out on them? They're just babies. Ashleigh starting school and Morgan starting her whole new life in this world.

He still didn't know how he made it through pre-school. Sian tried to help, but it got awkward. Sometimes it was weeks without speaking to another adult. Baby Singalong, soft play, adverts, health centre, even all the library books – it was mums this and mums that. Baby-change, always in the ladies'. The ultimate playground taunt? Your mum.

Dads weren't anywhere, not even as an insult. Even bloody Christmas was around a mum holding a baby. Joseph in the background like a mug.

But all that time, Ludi did know this: his girls would never have no one. He took on more jobs, but kept them local so he could get back in time. Maybe he spoilt them, but he'd rather go without so they could have the best. Was he trying to prove something? Definitely. All he ever wanted was for the girls to have more than him, to move up the ladder. Not down. The memories were like water from a burst pipe now.

When she was nine Ashleigh refused to wear a PE kit from Tesco, made him get one from the Gap. He acted annoyed, but was secretly glad, because she deserved it. And her Blackberry – she was the first kid in school to get one. That was when she turned ten. They'd had to move out the flat. She said she didn't want a birthday, just her old home back. That burned his actual heart when she said that. Things had been OK, though. He wasn't saying he was the perfect dad or anything. Maybe not the best dad in the world, but the best dad he knew.

Ludi jolted himself back into the present. It was now – he was nearly there, he had to be ready. He saw his reflection in a window and hardly knew himself. He puffed his cheeks up and let out a big breath. It was nearly the first delivery, and that was almost as sickening as plunging around in the past. Although the past was never past, he knew that now. Just like Scabby Mark's door today, same as it ever was.

And here he was. Ready now. This was the street, the first street. And here, the first of the front doors, staring at him. Wait, he panicked, I'm here already that was way too fast I'm not ready to do this. He stopped, reached inside his jacket. He wouldn't say anything. He looked up and down the road.

The first delivery would be the hardest – he just had to get it over with. He went through the garden gate, reached up his hand and pushed the doorbell. A woman opened the door – he recognised her: blonde, yoga-wear, like all the mums.

'Stacey? I'm Ashleigh's dad. She's been stealing and I have to give you this.' He awkwardly held the envelope out towards her. 'Sorry,' he said, and as she took it from him he turned and rushed away. It was done. He only noticed later that he caught his hand against the gate latch as he left. He felt the small trickle of blood a whole block later. He wiped it on his jeans. He looked around. Did anyone see? Was he talking? Don't look like a nutter. Gradually his feet slowed down.

The next one was only five minutes away. In normal life Ludi knocked on strangers' doors every day, and he was always welcome. Coming to the rescue – carrying his plumbing gear. Now without it he felt exposed, criminal. On to the next: Charlotte Dubree – he knew that name. Her daughter Lily-Mae teased Morgan about not having a mum. Wide white steps up to her front door, pots of flowers. But the person who answered the door and took the envelope wasn't her, it was a cleaning lady. Thank you, god. That wasn't so bad.

He set off again down the street again, and looked up to the trees overhead. The sky was moving behind. Could Ashleigh see this too? Trees, leaves, dust. Everything was made out of smaller things. Like me, he thought – it's only a small thing that I can do, what I'm doing, but even I can make it better. This time I can do it, Ash, I'm going to make it OK. It felt kind of like praying; maybe it was.

He checked his phone again. Still no message, no call. It was a bright ordinary day for everyone else. Just same old London all around him. Back on the pavement again, back out into this never-ending city that contained his children, his heart and soul. Walking onwards again like some ancient doomed person.

He had now handed over two packets of cash to mums robbed blind by his runaway outlaw of a daughter. There was one more to go. No wait, two more. It was blurring now, but he had got the hang of it. Faster, fast as possible. Instead of relief, though, Ludi felt a burst of fury. Which made no sense. But what the hell made sense any more?

38

ASHLEIGH GOES UP

It wasn't far from the back gates of the British Library back up to their area and to the summer school camp. Ashleigh wasn't running now. She got to the school's front gate and rang. 'Hi! I'm collecting Betsy – her mum asked me to come early?'

They buzzed her in. The grounds were empty, abandoned in the holidays, like a sunken ship. She had run and then walked so far that her feet were numb. But her eyes were very bright. She went into the toilets, sat down and greeted her own dazzling blood. She rolled a wad of tissue paper and stuffed it into her red-stained knickers. 'So much blood,' she hummed, and washed her hands and face.

She smoothed down her hair, tucked it behind her ears and walked round the corner to the sports hall. She was still burning red. But it was fine. The holiday-club kids were busy doing art, music and games. That was how it was – the world could carry on and tectonic plates would shift and planets move through space. Just the same. The play-scheme teacher recognised Ashleigh and did a thumbs-up. 'You here again! No rest for the wicked, am I right!'

Ashleigh smiled back at him, full beam. 'Got to make hay while the sun shines!' she replied. 'And the sun is shining! It's still shining,' she repeated it firmly, her smile fixed. He gave a puzzled look.

'I'm here for Betsy,' Ashleigh added. He turned and pointed at Betsy, sitting by herself.

Ashleigh stared. Of all the things I've taken, she thought, this is the only one I really want. Betsy looked across and her whole self lit up when she saw Ashleigh there. She ran over.

'Ashleigh!'

Ashleigh grabbed her by the hand. 'Betsy, we've got an adventure to go on – you'll never guess!'

'But I've got tennis.'

'Do you like tennis?'

Betsy zipped her bag closed. 'I hate tennis.'

'Oh wait – just a moment,' the teacher returned with an apologetic smile, 'I'll need to get parental authorisation for you to sign out – you're not listed for today, even though you've done all week – I know!' He rolled his eyes. 'Bear with me one moment while I call her mum.'

He went off to the phone in the corridor. 'Sure, no worries – I'm just going to take her to the toilet,' Ashleigh called after him, pulling Betsy along with her. They rounded the corner and then bolted for the school gate, Ashleigh pulling Betsy along by her hand, the girl's coat and bag hanging off her.

'What's happening?' Betsy laughed.

'Let's go! Your mum says it's fine. Come on!'

'But where are we going?'

'To my favourite place – my dream come true. Come on, let's go!' Ashleigh set off, laughing. 'No one else knows. Do you like the sound of that?'

'Yes! What dream?'

'Well, like a sleepover but different.'

'A sleepover! But I didn't bring a sleepover bag,' Betsy said, trotting along trying to keep up. 'My mum didn't say!'

CHAPTER 38

'Don't worry!' Ashleigh reached a hand out behind her. 'Come on! Let's go!'

Betsy grabbed tight on to the open hand just as they reached the school gate and together they half-ran, out and along the pavement. They were moving too fast for their usual meandering conversations. Betsy's glasses slipped down her nose as she struggled to keep up, her bag flapped and her jacket fell off her shoulder. Ashleigh's face was wildly bright as she pulled Betsy along, breathlessly urging her on.

'Look! It's the Hope bridge!' Ashleigh shouted. They ran side by side up the steps of the heavily graffitied bridge that crossed over the railway. Betsy looked up at her and her blonde hair flying around her head. She was very shiny.

'I don't need the stupid apple!' Ashleigh shouted on to the upwards wind.

'And I hate apples!' Betsy shouted, thrilled to join in. She didn't know what it meant but she laughed – they laughed together. Betsy didn't want this adventure to end – Ashleigh was like a girl in a book. She was like someone who could fly and was about to take off, to lift up into the sky.

'Haaaaaaah!' Ashleigh whooped, 'I love it!' Her mouth stayed open and Betsy could see her teeth. The two of them were above everything. They stood together at the top and peered through the railings to the tracks below. They didn't say anything. There was a metallic ringing sound as the rails crackled to life. A train was coming. Both girls trembled at the sound and looked at each other, eyes wide.

39

TARA CALLS

'I will make her pay for this.' Tara was shining with rage. 'I can literally never let a stranger into my house again.'

They were trapped in mutual disgust inside the freakish museum. Still no one was answering her calls. Holly looked away. How many miseries could she witness in one day? The garage doors behind them stood open, looking out to the short drive beside the front garden and on to the road and the world outside. There was sunlight on the outer twigs of the hedge.

'I think we have... a responsibility to reach Stacey and Charlotte,' Holly said, trying to use her work voice, 'but I still can't get through to her dad—' She took out her phone again.

'Responsibility?' Tara's voice rose. 'We're the victims here!' Her eyes widened. 'I feel totally violated, actually.'

'Victims?' Holly stood firm. 'She's underage, and we don't know where she is.'

She found the number again. She held up a hand as her phone connected. They listened. They heard the phone's tinny ringing sound break the flat solid silence of the garage. Then they heard it stop.

'And he just hung up on me,' she sighed, 'again.'

Tara jumped as her phone rang. 'Yes, that's me. What? WHAT?'

Her eyes widened and she turned her back on Holly as she spoke. 'When? She came early? You let my daughter go with Ashleigh?'

Holly froze.

'No! I did *not* authorise that – you have *not* heard the last of this—' Tara jabbed to end the call and turned to Holly. 'She's taken Betsy from summer school.'

For a second they stared at each other. 'Look, Ashleigh wouldn't hurt anyone – I'm sure Betsy will be fine,' Holly said. 'I'll keep calling her – probably her phone's just flat.'

But Tara wasn't listening. Her anger was only just getting started. 'I'll call Giles,' she said, her mouth tightening, a muscle twitching in her cheek as she looked at her phone. She raised the phone to her ear, her other hand clenched over her eyes. 'Giles.'

Holly stepped back slightly ahead of the tirade, and Tara's voice dropped so low it was almost a growl.

'He'll know what to do.'

40

SCABBY MARK SMILES AGAIN

Scabby Mark was in his good chair, skinning up in front of the telly. He'd had his soup and *Neighbours* was starting soon. It was working out all right if Ludi came through as a new delivery guy. With his own van! Not a bad day. He whistled the *Neighbours* theme tune, rolling up the tip into a twist. Nice and tidy. Where was his lighter?

His work phone went. He stretched out one leg, patted his trackie pockets and reached in. He turned it over and looked at the screen. He stood up to answer but his roach and the Rizla pack rolled off his lap and fell on the floor. He grabbed down to rescue them off the rug and tried to answer at the same time, but accidentally put it to voicemail instead.

'Shit!' he grunted as he left them there and gradually stood up again, wondering whether to call back, or wait and see if there was a message.

He looked at the screen. Giles. That's funny, he thought. It's only been a week – why's he calling me again so soon? Had he noticed there was a bit less than usual? Should I call him back? Before he could decide the voicemail rang and he picked up. 'You have... *one*... new message.' He stooped as he listened, trying to pick the roach back out of the scattered shreds of tobacco on his rug.

CHAPTER 40

'Mark, it's me, Giles. Bit of an emergency.' The voice burst out of his phone like it was on loudspeaker. 'Need to find someone from your block. She's stolen from us. That girl Ashleigh. Call me back.'

Click.

Ashleigh? He did know her! That was Ludi's girl. But why would someone like Giles know someone like her? His pulse was rising as he called the number back. It was answered immediately.

'Yes?'

'All right, Giles, it's... it's me. What can I do you for? Haha!'

'Do you know her?'

'OK, Ashleigh, yeah, that's Ludi's girl, yeah, I know who you mean.'

'Find her. It's urgent.'

Scabby Mark blew his cheeks out silently. Never heard the posh boy like this before. Suddenly sounding like the bad guy in *Die Hard*. He smiled.

'No problem, sure, yeah, I see that one all the time, always heading in and out the place.' He turned his hand round and picked at the long nail of his little finger. 'You won't believe this, right, he was here this morning, was her dad!' He almost sat back down in his chair as he spoke, then decided to stay standing up. He scratched his belly with satisfaction. 'Asking to sign up – he wants to work with me! We've entered into a little business arrangement as it happens.'

'What?' Giles interrupted.

'Ludi. He's all right,' Scabby Mark rubbed his neck as he made his way round his flat to the open balcony door. 'He knows everyone round here, he's good. I could call him up and see if he knows where she is? He's got a van!'

He looked out into the balcony as he spoke. It was turning into the most exciting day since that massive raid upstairs. The one where they got the wrong flat. And now here was Giles on the phone, and he was asking for help. 'We need to know where she is *now*.' And his voice really did sound weird. For a second Scabby Mark wondered if this was a spoof, a prank call that would end in a burst of laughter. But it didn't.

'Can you see her?' He stepped outside holding his phone in one hand and his Rizlas in the other, looking out over his balcony wall and down below. That Ashleigh girl was nowhere to be seen. Some mums with buggies were sat watching their toddlers and a girl in an Arsenal strip was playing keepy-uppy with a ball.

'Hold on,' he said, leaning out and looking closer, squinting down.

'What? Is she there – can you see her?'

'OK, it's sorted, Giles.' He was smiling again. 'I know how to get her.'

41

MORGAN GOES TO THE
FIFTH FLOOR

Morgan was playing down in the square. At the sleepover they had pancakes for breakfast and then she came home, but no one was there and now she was bored. She stepped outside and some of the bad kids went by but she ignored them and they ignored her back.

Ashleigh always told her to stay away and that they got their new bikes by being bad and she mustn't talk to them. Morgan didn't want to talk to them, anyway – they were good at wheelies but sucked at football. She was going to wait for Kalia and Majid to come down. Their mum was making them eat lunch.

She was practising her kick-ups, and counting under her breath. Seven, eight, nine... She had her new football boots on – they were going to be so jealous. She wasn't going to even say anything about them, she planned, just be already training in them when they came down. They'd go mad!

She got all the way to ten kick-ups, and then eight twice in a row. In her year she was the best dribbler, and in the top three fastest runners including the boys. Her highest kick-ups score was seventeen, but that was in the corridor and no one saw. Five, six, seven... she was counting under her breath when there was a noise overhead. She let the ball fall; it rolled away. She looked up.

'Oi! Up here!' someone was shouting down off a balcony. She shaded her eyes and looked all the way up at the person leaning over a high-up wall. She looked behind herself on both sides and then back up at him.

'Yes, you!' he called. 'I've got something that was your mum's. Come up!'

Morgan knew about paedos. They'd been taught at school, and Ashleigh always said not to talk to anyone in the street or the kids on bikes or anyone on the block apart from the people they knew. That was before, though. Now Ashleigh never talked to her.

She stood still. 'What?' she called back.

'Come up – fifth floor – something for you!'

She stared. Dad said they couldn't go to the fifth floor, but even he didn't know about the haunted door where there used to be a witch but she died. Majid said it was true, because the cats were still there who had eaten her. But no one would see if she went up and came straight back down quickly. Morgan picked up her ball and ran to the stairs. No one ever talked about her mum. She used to ask Ash how their mum died, but Ash always said shut up. Dad wouldn't ever say. And no one else asked – not since they drew family trees in school. She was sat next to Lily-Mae, who looked and said, 'That's not a tree, it's a tiny little bush.' And Morgan never got told off for punching her, so she knew people weren't allowed to ask. But she didn't know why.

So Morgan went up the stairs, past her own floor, then two more. She'd never been on the fifth floor – not even for a dare. She looked back, down and up the stairwell – there was no one else around. Ashleigh wouldn't like this, and Dad wouldn't like this. But they weren't here. She started along the corridor, bouncing her ball the whole way until she reached the open door. She caught the ball and held it in front of her in both hands. She looked inside.

'Hello?'

'Did you know I knew your mum?' Scabby Mark looked up from the sofa and smiled. 'She used to come up here and visit me, just like this!'

Morgan hesitated in the doorway.

'Don't be shy – it's fine! We're neighbours, aren't we?' He shuffled all his smoking things to one side then stood up. 'Come on in and sit down and I can tell you about your mum.' He scratched his back. 'And it's funny because your dad was here today as well.'

'You've got something from her? How?' Morgan said, not moving. She saw his flaky eyes, his hair hanging down at the back. He looked sort of wet and dry at the same time. He smiled some more.

'Ah, look at you – nice T-shirt. Proper little Gooner, aren't you?' He took a step towards her. She looked back out into the corridor then back to him. His eyelids were red. What was he going to say about her mum? But what if Ash found out she was here? Morgan didn't speak or even move.

'Yeah, your dad was here,' he carried on. 'Asked me for a job, he did! And now look – here you are! Did you know that? Did you know your dad's working for me now? But listen, we need to know where your sister is.' He smiled encouragingly and leant forward. 'Where's Ashleigh?'

She frowned and jutted her chin up. She rolled the ball between her hands with the exact same level stare as her older sister. 'You didn't know my mum!'

He grinned and moved closer. 'Oh, lots of people knew your mum! She had some special friends up here. Very special.' He giggled. 'But what people don't know is – she didn't die!'

Morgan's hands gripped the ball. Her mouth was open.

'I know! Doesn't everyone think she died?' Scabby Mark was delighted by the changing expressions on the girl's face. 'Well, she didn't! But – call up your sister,' he said, remembering to be serious again. 'It's urgent – we've got to find her.'

'She… she…' Morgan couldn't get her words out.

'You're only young, but everyone deserves to hear the truth!'

'You're lying!' Morgan's face went red, even her neck.

He looked down at her, his mouth curled. 'And you need to learn some respect. Call your sister.' He pulled out his phone and waggled it in her face, moving closer. 'Call her! People are looking for her, you know, so you better help.' He moved again. 'We can't talk with you by the door. Come here.'

He reached round her back as if to herd her into the room, but she recoiled, raising her elbow sharply, which knocked his hand outwards and his phone fell on the carpet.

'Shit,' he said, darting forward to block her way with a squeaky laugh. 'What are you doing? It's fine, stop—' He pushed her with his forearm, still laughing a forced laugh.

'Call your sister!'

He moved again, blocking and shoving her backwards into the room, and now it felt like slow motion as she shouted, 'No! I'm telling my dad!'

'Shut your mouth!' He wasn't laughing now.

He reached his hand towards her face, but she lunged forwards and bit him. Her bared teeth caught on to the inside of his arm, but he shook so hard her head flipped back.

212

'No!' She screamed it this time, ducking under his arm as he swore and turned his wrist, and she ran to the door and back out into the corridor. Her ball was rolling on the floor. There was only the sound of her steps running away.

'Little bitch!' he shouted after her. His wrist was bleeding. 'No wonder your mum left!'

He pinched the skin closed, eyes watering with pain.

42

BETSY HOPES

'Ashleigh! Ashleigh!'

She was with Ashleigh, they were together up high on top of the bridge, when the shouts reached their ears. Betsy looked down and saw Samina, shouting from the street below. Samina, the babysitter from before – number six. Maybe she was coming back. Betsy hoped she wasn't coming to take Ashleigh's place. Samina caught the railing at the bottom of the steps and hurried up towards them. The steps made a clanging metallic echo.

'I was hoping I'd see you!'

Samina stopped and stood in front of the pair, looking intently from one to the other. Betsy saw Ashleigh let go of the iron railings and reach down for her hand. Betsy took the hand, and she gave it an extra squeeze that was like a reminder that they both hated apples and so that Ashleigh would know she still wanted to do the sleepover even though she didn't have a sleepover bag.

Betsy saw Samina looking at their joined hands. 'Hi!' Samina said. 'And how are you?' She bent forward towards Betsy, who frowned and moved closer to Ashleigh. With her free hand Betsy put up her jacket hood, then straightened her glasses. She was in between two babysitters – the old one and her new one. It made Ashleigh seem less magic and powerful. It wasn't good.

214

'Hello, Samina,' she said.

'I've missed you,' Samina said, smiling down at her. 'But it looks like you're in safe hands – right, Ashleigh!' But Ashleigh didn't speak at all. And now Betsy could see that her cheeks and neck were wet with tears and some of them had plopped on to the front of her rainbow T-shirt. But her face didn't look like she was crying. And Samina wasn't acting like she was talking to a crying person. Betsy wished Samina would go back down the steps, go away and leave them alone.

'I've been working on case notes for my letter to Tara,' she said, lugging her shoulder bag round to show them. 'I don't know if you heard, but she accused me of stealing and I got a police warning.'

'OK.' Ashleigh shrugged.

'Obviously that threatened my law degree.'

Ashleigh swallowed. Betsy felt a shaking in the hand she was holding, and when she looked up at Ashleigh's face it had changed again and looked different. Another train ran underneath the bridge with a rush of upwards air and a stream of rhythmic clanging and rattling sounds. Gradually they began to fade out. Samina kept her eyes on Ashleigh. Betsy felt like no one could see her any more, like she wasn't there. As the train noises faded Ashleigh lifted up Betsy's hand and flapped it in an awkward wave saying, 'OK, well we were on our way…'

'Some money went missing, apparently,' Samina went on, looking at Ashleigh.

There was another long pause. Ashleigh looked back. Betsy looked from one staring face to the other, but neither of them looked down at her. Then Ashleigh dropped Betsy's hand and her arms hung by her sides. Her head was down and a little bit to the side, then she looked as though she was about to say something when Samina carried on.

'I'm a law student – well, I was a law student – and with a little help from this' – she pulled a white envelope half way out of her bag and showed them – 'I can clear my name, get myself back together.'

Ashleigh frowned as Samina tucked it away again.

'What is that?'

'It's a legal letter. I'm on my way to give it to Tara.'

'OK, what for?'

'The letter? Not revenge. I'm after something better than that. I want Justice.'

'Not pretentious at all!' Ashleigh rolled her eyes. Betsy didn't know what this meant and looked to Samina to see if she was annoyed. But all she did was take a step forward and lean in much closer, dropping her voice right down.

'I'm allowed to sound pretentious, Ashleigh – last week I was on the edge too.'

Then she did a kind of special stare at Ashleigh. It was like the one her mum used in shops, and Betsy didn't like it.

'What?' Ashleigh's voice jumped up. 'No! I wasn't—'

'I've been thinking about you.' Samina stepped back again.

'What?' Ashleigh's eyes narrowed in the sun.

'Ashleigh. Are you OK?'

'I… I don't know. No,' Ashleigh said. She sounded like she was pushing her voice out. 'No one's ever asked me.'

Footsteps echoed as a man came pounding up the steps of the bridge talking on a hands-free phone: 'Yes it is!' And it's not about the marginals, Jeremy – you've got to forget about that!' He chopped the air with both hands and didn't register the three figures standing there. In silence they watched him pass by. As he clattered down the other side of the bridge Samina took a breath and tried again.

'Listen. My mum used to have these sayings, and they pretty much kept me going when she died. My favourite was about how we don't live alone, we are one body. I don't know how to explain it.' Samina looked away over the bridge with a longing smile. 'It might feel like you're on your own, Ashleigh, but you're not. You're not!'

Betsy nodded at this and looked up to Ashleigh for agreement. But Ashleigh was blank. The magic Ashleigh from before wasn't there now. Betsy felt all of her fingers close tightly together and looked down at the ground. She had watched their faces for almost the whole time on top of the bridge, apart from when the shouting man came, and she had followed all the words. At first she could understand them – it had seemed OK. But now it wasn't. She got the tired feeling of wanting to hide away.

Samina patted her bag and stepped back. 'I'm on my way – got work to do!' She looked close into Ashleigh's face again. 'But if you ever want to talk…'

'Samina,' Ash hesitated. She was quiet now, and smaller, the shining powers had vanished. 'I never knew that it would hurt you – what I did.' She looked down and her cheeks went pink. 'I wish I hadn't. And if you're going to see Tara, you could tell her that…' She took a deep breath. 'That you know everything that I know. That you know about his problems at work… his *situation*. And her *trainer*. Just that. If you want.'

Betsy gathered up the effort and managed to push her voice in between them. 'Situation?'

'Oh – sorry!'

'Nothing!'

They both looked down at her and replied at the same time and then laughed in a jokey grown-ups way and smiled at each other. This gave Betsy the feeling she always had at school. She and Ashleigh weren't special any more, now that the two babysitters had turned into a team together and she was outside of it. She pressed her fingertips together.

Samina carried on. 'Well, I don't think I will tell her that… But thanks anyway!'

On top of this a new sound burst in – a squawking ringtone. 'That's Morgan!' Ashleigh dug in her pocket. 'Wait.' She rushed and scrambled to answer. 'Morgan?' There was some sobbing, strange bad noises – it sounded like a cat on the other end of the call.

'Morgan – Morgan?' Betsy couldn't understand anything now, apart from it was all making Ashleigh more far away from her. Everything had gone bad. She gave up trying to look at their faces and listen to the sounds, and instead she looked down at the ground and the glittery surface of the bridge and the graffiti and pictures all along, and the dirt in the edges where a very tiny plant was growing in the crack. It had two blue flowers.

'He said what? *Are you OK?* Our mum what?' Ashleigh span away to the side. 'I'm coming.'

Ashleigh's voice had changed again, and this time it sounded more like a mum kind of voice. 'I'm coming home now.' She turned back round to face them and her eyes had gone dark and big and her face wasn't pink any more but of light grey colour.

'I have to go – it's my sister. Something's happened!'

'Go! Go!' Samina moved forwards quickly. 'Listen, I can take Betsy home for you – since I'm going there anyway?'

Betsy bunched her hands inside her pockets, especially the hand that Ashleigh had been holding. She pressed her thumbnails into each finger in turn, then did it in reverse. Ashleigh had a real sister of her own, and now she was going away. And now Ashleigh was crouching down in front of her, trying to look at her.

'Bye, Betsy,' she whispered.

Betsy said nothing. She backed away. She pulled her hood tighter over her ears. Ashleigh turned and ran.

43

LUDI RUNS IN THE WRONG DIRECTION

There were still two more deliveries left to do, and they were the worst ones. This next one, oh no, Ludi groaned. Especially after all the digging up of the past. He knew this pavement too well. He knew its kerbs and cracks from pushing the buggy along. He knew which front gardens could distract a slow-walking toddler. He was going to their old place, his old home. It's not the same neighbourhood it was when we lived here, he thought. Or maybe it was him who had changed?

No, his old London was eaten up on every side. Look at these houses – who lives in them? Even the flats round Tanghall were getting bought up by rich people or people from somewhere else. People who were faster. He was too slow. What if his kids had kids? There'd be no place for them here. London's only got space for violin-playing children, is that it? What about the just normal ones. Even if this was still his neighbourhood, it wouldn't be theirs.

No, he was the same person. It was the world that had got tougher. And so had Ashleigh. Thank god for Morgan. The thought of her made him smile, that fierce little thing, always keeping up like small dog that doesn't know it's small. She still loved her dad, and they played footy every weekend. A new pain came at the thought of expensive football boots, not to mention she was already begging for the new Arsenal away strip, the purple and black.

But now he'd gone backwards, now he could see how good it was before and he hadn't known that that was good, that they were winning, that he was making it better. Look at him now, working for Scabby Mark. The shame stabbed his insides. These packets of cash were two things – the end of him, and a start for Ashleigh. How the hell he would climb out of this was for another time. But one day he'd take Morgan to the Emirates Stadium.

He straightened, firmed up by this ambition, but still keeping his eyes down. He felt his face start to burn when he got close to Nicky's house again. Shut out that memory. Walk normally, he told himself, pull yourself together! He couldn't look up at old Nicky's house, or those garage doors. Then here was their old front garden – he remembered Steve's van waiting outside, he remembered coming out right here.

Stop remembering and just get on with it, he decided – memories haven't helped, they haven't answered anything. The gate was open. So many of these people had gates, and it was like they were already judging you before you even got to the front door. He walked up – it looked quiet; maybe no one was at home. Maybe he could just delay it and try again later. He paused. He rang the bell.

Felt like he'd been knocking at fucking doors all day. This was just another one. He stood there, he shuffled in his jacket. His old home. The front door was new, though – smooth grey paint. He'd thrown the keys into Camden Lock that dark mad night. Not himself, just the keys.

There was a noise inside and then the door opened and there she was: Tara. Big eyes and a red mouth and shiny hair. Standing there in her own doorway – it was her house now, all of it. She was frowning and holding the door with one hand. The other held a phone to her ear.

She did an irritable 'What?' face at him. But he was prepared. He reached it out to her, then the envelope was in her hand.

'I'm Ashleigh's dad.'

Her mouth fell open, her eyes popped wide, she looked down at the envelope in her hand.

'That's to make up for... It's – uh, compensation.'

Tara snapped into her phone, 'I'll call you back.'

But Ludi was already halfway back to the gate.

'Stop!' shouted Tara. He looked back and her neck was bulging like it was full of cables.

'I'm sorry—' He was at the gate. 'I've got to—'

'She won't get away with this!' she screamed, and louder, 'She's got my girl! She's got my daughter! Where is she? I'm about to call the police – I am seriously about to call them—'

'No!'

'What about my girl?' She stepped out of the door towards him with her bright pink toenails on the path. 'Where is she?'

What the fuck was she on about? Ludi reeled, grabbing tight on to the gatepost. What about *my* girl? He turned back into the stream of words and she was still at it – 'Your daughter's a psycho! She will pay for this!'

'I'm trying—' He got himself through the gate and in his panic he ran off in the wrong direction. He turned the corner and stopped, fists bunched, chest heaving. She was a bad woman, gaping mouth, pointy eyes. Knew one when he saw one. All the old fear came back. He could hear her voice turning raw, and her words chased after him: 'I will make her pay!'

He leant on the wall, shaking, his bones and heart suddenly full of the deepest tiredness, and it was much more than the sleepless nights with a sick child or the long days of work. He felt tired, like he could lie down on the pavement and stop. What in god's name had Ashleigh done now? It was a nightmare that refused to end – he couldn't keep rescuing her from things he didn't understand. He had nothing left. No way out. No plan B. Nothing.

Then his phone buzzed. His hands moved clumsily as he turned it over to look. And there – there was her name. It was her. It was Ashleigh.

44

SAMINA WINS

It was strange not to have a key, but Samina felt calmer than she'd ever felt in front of this door. She and Betsy had been holding hands until she knocked. Then she let Betsy's hand go, pulled the folder out of her bag and brought out the large white envelope. A moment later Tara tore the door wide open; her hair was sticking out and her eyes swivelled between Samina and Betsy in confusion. Her face was livid. Before Tara could settle into her default anger Samina moved forwards, gently patting Betsy's back as they stepped inside, and spoke.

'Hi, Tara, I brought Betsy back,' she said. They were in the hallway, with Tara reversing before them, still speechless. 'And you have to revoke the police warning.'

'Betsy! My darling – what – oh my god – where…' Tara burst into words and flapped movements. 'Betsy, go upstairs! I love you! Wait, how the hell have—'

'This is my legal deposition,' said Samina, interrupting her and handing the pages over. 'This is your copy. Read it.'

'Betsy, darling – now, please!' Tara pulled the sheets of paper out of the envelope. 'Take your jacket off! Upstairs!'

Betsy didn't look at either of them. She kept her jacket on with her hood pulled tightly around her face. She made a growling noise and stomped her way up the stairs, dropped her bag on the floor and slammed her bedroom door. Samina watched her, then turned back to face Tara.

Tara glanced at the papers despite herself. She seemed to be caught between wanting to take a look and not wanting to do as she'd just been told. She was now holding them in one hand, the other hand on her hip as though she was about to deliver a lecture. Samina stood firm. It felt so good that this person was no longer her boss.

'It's all set out – here, look,' she said, pointing. 'You will go to the police and revoke that warning in person so I can go back to my studies.'

Tara looked down at the papers with a small shrug as though it was a piece of junk mail for a pizza delivery service that she would now have to go to the effort of putting in the recycling. Samina didn't let this diminish her. One of her law professors had once talked about the 'tell' being the moment a witness gives themself away with an unconscious movement. They think they're lying successfully to your face but suddenly you can read it. Samina wasn't sure exactly how, but she could see something now that she had never seen before. It was something she hadn't known she could even hope for. She could see that Tara had lost.

'Also, Tara,' Samina went on, 'these things you do to people, the destruction—'

'What are you talking about, "destruction"?' Tara interrupted. 'That's just ridiculous!'

Tara got her energy from anger, Samina remembered. She paused. Maybe she could frame it in a way that would make someone like Tara understand.

'The way you treat people, it's kind of like vandalism – you're like the person who snaps off the saplings.'

'*What?*'

'The new trees – the council plants them but someone keeps snapping them. They're just trying to grow!'

Tara snorted and looked to the side in disbelief.

Samina quickly changed strategies. 'Another thing, Tara. Don't quote me in your blogs or I will sue you.'

'OK, great. Noted, Samina!' Tara held up the papers in her hand and did her big-eyed smile. '*Well done* with those law studies!' She had the air of a politician confronted with a constituent of below-average intelligence. 'And thank you for dropping Betsy off. Was there anything else?'

'Yes.' Samina decided to try out one more line of attack. After all, she was here right now, and Tara had lost. Even if she didn't know it yet. She took a breath and balanced her weight evenly on both feet. 'Whatever it is that you intend to do to Ashleigh, because of what she… *knows*… I strongly suggest that you don't.'

It was a bluff. Samina had never done anything like this before, and she didn't have the faintest idea how it might work. And it was so entirely delicious that she almost trembled. Tara's face stopped, her hand flew up and she touched the corners of her mouth. Then she licked her lips.

'You know?'

And Samina couldn't resist. 'Yes. I know.'

45

LUDI TALKS

Buzzing. Buzzing. Ludi stared at this phone. This time it was her. At last it was her! After all the fear, and the missed calls. Here she was at last, she was here. Ludi stopped and his heart stopped and he looked to the sky. There was nothing there. He held his phone up steadily and pressed answer. He paused before he spoke and then quietly said, 'Ashleigh.'

'Dad?'

'Ashleigh, thank god!' It all came tumbling out. 'OK, I want you to know it's sorted – I've sorted it. You don't need to—'

'Dad. Morgan says the guy upstairs told her about Mum – that Mum – that…' Ashleigh's breathing sounded like she was running.

'What?'

'That Mum's not dead, that she's alive.'

'What! What guy?' His thoughts rushed up and down. 'Is Morgan OK? What guy?'

'Up on the fifth floor. I'm going to her now – I'm almost home. Dad – why?'

'Was it Scabby Mark? I said never go up there! I told you both—'

'You told us she was dead.'

'I didn't! I just – I – it was less bad,' he stammered. 'It was easier to let everyone – Ash? I'm coming home – we can talk…'

He waited, but she said nothing. He looked at the phone, then pressed the phone closer to his ear. He was still standing in the middle of the pavement. He couldn't hear anything. He rubbed his head.

'Ash? I've fixed it – I got money to pay the families – you can go home – I've paid Tara, and we can sort out all that – that stuff, it's all fixed.'

This last part all came out in a rush, but still Ashleigh didn't say anything. 'I've paid them, Ashleigh.' His voice went higher. 'I've done it.' He rubbed his head again. 'Ashleigh?'

46

ASHLEIGH COMES HOME

Ashleigh moved steadily, swiftly like she was on rails, curving the edges of the blocks and eating up the space between her and her sister. Faster and faster. She was back at Tanghall and their block in no time, and she ran straight up the stairs. As she turned the corner before their floor she stopped at the sight of her sister, sitting on the step at the end of their corridor with her arms round her knees.

When she caught sight of Ashleigh, Morgan's mouth opened wide and she started crying with her whole body. Ashleigh ran to her, sitting next to her and gathering her in. Morgan pressed her face into her sister.

'He got me, he tried to catch me,' she cried.

'I'm here now,' Ashleigh soothed, and held her, stroking her hair. The sight of her, her smallness, the top of her head. She smelt of love. That's when the movement came inside, Ashleigh's neck released, her heart untightened. Her sister's voice came flooding into her. And all those times came back, the times when Ash would carry her baby sister around. Her sister was crying, and it gushed into Ashleigh's heart. She shut her eyes and held Morgan tight.

'I hate him, that bastard man!' Morgan leant into Ashleigh's body.

'Shh, Morgan, let's go in.'

'The bad man, upstairs,' she cried, 'he's after you, he's looking for you!'

'Let's go inside.'

'And it was my fault!'

'Morgan, it was my fault. But it's going to be OK. Come here.' Ashleigh hoisted Morgan up to her feet, shocked by the full weight of her sister. She hadn't held her for – it must be years. Morgan's face was puffed up and there was a streak of spit near her mouth. Ashleigh wiped it away. They were still on the step at the end of the corridor, and Morgan's arms were round her waist, crying into the front of her T-shirt. Ashleigh held her for a longer time. Her not-yet-formed sister, her flesh and blood, her pure undamaged girl, her very own. A fierce love surged inside Ashleigh and it felt stronger than rage. She spoke as gently as she could. 'Morgan,' she said, stroking her sister's hair back, 'what happened?'

Morgan held tighter and spoke into Ashleigh's belly, her face squashed into the front of her T-shirt. 'He said why didn't we know that our mum is still alive!'

Ashleigh felt that beat inside herself again, a thudding noise, a dropping of her insides.

'He said no she's not dead and why did we think that,' she cried. 'Ashy, what does it mean?'

'Don't worry. I love you.'

'And I... I...' Morgan's body shook. 'I'm sorry I... I...'

'What?' Ashleigh clutched her. 'It's OK! Morgan! What happened? Did he touch you?'

'I left my ball behind!' she sobbed with complete abandon.

Ashleigh rocked her sister, and she felt an old power. 'Morgan. I'll get you a new ball. That man's just an old druggy loser. He doesn't know anything.' She squeezed her tighter and closer. 'Let's go home.'

They left the step and went along the corridor to their own front door. Their flat was small, but once the door shut behind them it was safe. She led Morgan to the sofa. At the side Ashleigh saw Ludi's bedding folded up. It gave her a pinching feeling. They sat down and leant together, feeling the warmth and their bodies were closer than they had been for a long time. Morgan sniffed and kept her face down, then she took a shuddering breath.

'Ashy, and I'm sorry about the apple, Ash.' Her voice became panicky and ragged again. She gulped. 'I'm really sorry, I didn't know.'

Ashleigh had a terrible flashback to their fight, the big fight. Morgan had taken the apple from under Ashleigh's pillow and tried to hide it under her own. 'It's something to do with Mum, isn't it! Why won't you tell me!' she had shouted, 'Tell me! Tell me!' and Ashleigh had attacked her.

She felt sick recalling the sight of her sister's pulled hair sticking out at the side, remembering how stupid she looked as she cried, and screaming at her, 'I hate you! I wish it was you who was dead instead of her!' The memory raked up Ashleigh's insides. She swallowed and closed her eyes against the shame.

'Come here.' She pulled Morgan in; even their bones leant against each other. 'Please don't think about the apple. That's not... anything any more. I don't know what got into me.'

The photos, the sofa, walls, blanket, everything around them was comfy and safe.

'Anyway, she could've found us if she wanted to,' Ashleigh mumbled.

'What?' Morgan looked up. Ashleigh was staring straight ahead. 'Ashy?'

Ashleigh snapped back into the moment. She looked back down at her sister. 'Right now it's just us, and that's enough for me.' She caught hold of Morgan's hand and squeezed it tightly, then pulled it towards her mouth and growled and pretended to gnaw on it like a bone. Morgan laughed and squirmed. Then she looked up again.

'You don't want to go and live with Tara?'

'Oh my god, are you actually kidding me?' Ashleigh gave a small demented laugh. 'Listen, I love you and so does Dad. He'd do anything for us, Morgy.'

She reached over and pulled a blanket off Ludi's bedding pile, wrapped it all around Morgan and tucked her in, then piled a cushion on top. 'I'm making you a hot chocolate. Dad'll be here soon.'

Ashleigh went over to the kitchen area. She shrugged off her jacket with her phone inside the pocket. She hung it on the chair and turned away. She leant against the wall with her eyes half shut while the kettle boiled. The steam touched her face. Two spoons of chocolate powder in each mug and the hot water. It smelt sweet. And a bit of milk. She stirred mechanically, watching the powdery lumps spinning around and shrinking.

Solubility is a measurement of how much of a substance will dissolve in a given volume of a liquid, she said inside her head, and dropped the spoon in the sink. She carried the drinks through and placed them on the stool by the sofa. Things dissolve and they turn into something else. She turned on the TV and switched through to the kids' channel.

Morgan hadn't moved, bundled up inside the fleecy blanket. Ashleigh looked at her as if she hadn't seen her in ages, looked at her brown hair, her round cheeks, her thick eyebrows, her Arsenal t-shirt. Then she sat down and pushed in next to her on the sofa, reached over and pulled the blanket over both their knees. She gathered her sister up again, kissed her on top of her head, held her. And Morgan's warm weight made her feel surrounded all round, like a bird inside its nest.

47

HOLLY PULLS

Holly lifted her keyboard to shake out the crumbs. Her cheese and salad-cream roll was stuffed with cheese and onion crisps – the Holly Special, her colleagues called it, but it made a right mess when you put the crisps in. She'd come in late after all that crazy drama in the morning and was trying to catch her workload up. Three empty mugs staked the desk boundaries and her potted plant drooped so badly they were saying she'd be put on the offenders' register.

Her phone buzzed, its vibrations dancing over the desk top. She turned it over.

Im here outside, can u meet

Her pulse quickened and she looked around as though she'd done something wrong. She slid the phone into her pocket, stood up and announced vaguely to the office, 'Back in a minute.' She ran outside and along the corridor to their kitchen where she made two mugs of tea. She decided against the I'm Sexy And I Know It mug in favour of one with a pug. She carried them downstairs and towards the glass front of the building. She paused near reception, a mug in each hand, near the security barriers. She looked out. There he was on

233

the other side, sitting on a low wall in the sun. His face looked tight. He was sort of hugging himself.

She wrangled her ID card out and swiped through the barriers. She prepared a smile as she stepped out into the sunshine. She walked over and sat down next to Ludi. 'All right! I brought you a brew. You probably need one after this morning!'

'Uh,' he kept looking down, 'I can't stay.'

'Two sugars,' she said, holding the mug out. It wasn't a question. 'Have you heard from Ashleigh?'

'Yes.'

'And?'

'I think it's going to be OK.'

Ludi paused, then rearranged his arms so he was hugging himself with one hand, and reached out for the tea with the other. Holly pretended not to notice this awkwardness, put the remaining cup down and adjusted the angle of her body so they were both looking ahead, side by side.

'I tried to call you.'

'I know,' said Ludi, putting his tea down on the wall. 'I've sorted it – I've paid them. The other mums. On the parent list you shared.'

Holly looked at him. Ludi was staring down. A siren passed by. London moved around them as they sat motionless on the wall. He drew in a breath.

'Yeah. Apart from one... So here you go.'

Ludi reached inside his jacket and pulled out an envelope. He shoved it sideways at Holly. She held it in both hands. She turned it over but didn't open it. Behind it she could see their feet in a row next to each other. Holly's work shoes, her smart ones from M&S. Ludi's trainers, his feet turned inwards and resting on their sides. She glanced up to his hands, the hairs on his wrists.

CHAPTER 47

'Ludi?' She wanted to turn and face him, to touch his arm. But the worst thing would be to show kindness – it could open up the floodgates and Ludi might dissolve. She'd seen his pain. No one wants to be seen suffering like that. Be professional, she told herself, and let him hold himself together. She looked inside the envelope, poked a finger inside. 'Bloody hellfire! Where did you…?'

Ludi looked away down the street. Holly fingered through the wad of purple twenties, her mouth open, her face incredulous. She glanced from side to side then at Ludi. 'It's too much!'

'But – the things in the garage, all that stuff…' He looked back at her. 'And you sent me their details,' he frowned. 'What did you think I was doing?'

Holly took her gaze away and squinted into the sunlight. Then looked down again and ruffled through the notes. 'She took £72, so I'll take that, not a penny more. I'll have this eighty… here… and you take this lot back… or have you got any change? Hold on a minute – I think I've got some…'

Holly filled the space up with words and made a big deal of rooting around in her bag chattering about how she thought there was some change in here somewhere, wait a minute, there now, if I give you this fiver then oh yes here's one, two, three and then we're good.

She zipped her bag closed. It was done. She felt like a transaction had taken place that she didn't fully understand. She wanted to be on the same side as him, but now it felt like she wasn't. For a moment they looked at each other while people walked past on the street, phones rang, traffic moved and the sun shone its ordinary light. Holly's hair moved in the breeze; she tried to tuck it behind her ear, looked away, and then back at Ludi.

'It's so hard, isn't it,' she said.

'What?' he looked defensive.

'I mean, what do I know? I've only got one – but I often think, do we ever really know our children?'

'Wrong person to ask.' Ludi said grimly. 'But maybe it's not our job to know them – just to… just… be there. I don't know.'

Holly smiled. She couldn't tell why that made her feel sad.

'OK, see you later.' Ludi stood up and turned, ready to go. His face had an animal determination, like a swimming dog. The mugs still sat on the wall.

Holly didn't want to go back into the office. She blurted out, 'I'm feeling well flush now – we should meet later for a pint!' and laughed nervously. He turned back to look at her. There was a silence. Shit – what had got into her? Her face felt hot.

He seemed to think it over then replied, 'You'll be wanting a different babysitter, though.'

There was a beat before Holly saw he was teasing her. 'All right, OK!' She panicked inside, trying to think of something funny to say back.

'I better go,' he said, and started to stand up. 'But – thanks for the tea. Sorry I…' He took a quick gulp then put the mug down next to hers. 'I've got to go.'

'No no, it's fine, you head off!'

'I'll call you?'

Holly nodded and he walked away. She picked up the mugs so it didn't look like she was watching him leave. She tried not to smile. She was such an idiot, really. She couldn't stop the smile from escaping. She looked again and double-checked that he was gone, then lifted up his mug and took a sip from it. Her smile was still there. She really should head back in now.

48

LUDI GETS HOME

CBeebies *Bedtime Hour* was on TV, with *Story Makers*, with the friendly yellow blobs and Blue Cow. The colours and the happy songs washed over the two girls, tangled up on the sofa. Morgan's legs were across Ashleigh's lap when their dad came in the door. He landed heavily next to them, like he was like the last runner to cross the finishing line.

No one said anything. Morgan slurped her hot chocolate, one hand clamped around her sister's fingers.

The presenters came on, wearing their pyjamas. 'It's time for the good night story, children!'

'Dad.' Ashleigh's eyes were on the TV. 'Why didn't you tell us?'

Ludi sank down a bit further, keeping his eyes down.

'That she's… not… dead.' Ashleigh's voice was on one level and didn't go up or down. 'Why…?'

'Because she – because she didn't want us.' Ludi's voice was soft. 'She didn't want us. She never did. But I do – I,' he put a hand over his eyes and swallowed, 'I love us.'

Ashleigh didn't say anything. Morgan's fingers tightened around Ashleigh's hand and squeezed.

'I should've told you. I got that… wrong…'

It was quiet. And then Ludi stretched out one arm – he reached it round Ashleigh's back. She didn't shake him off. He breathed out and shut his eyes.

'Good night, moon and stars, good night.' The presenters waved their teddy bears.

'Dad...' Ashleigh bent her head down, hid her face in her sister's hair. Her voice was muffled. 'I don't... I don't know...'

'Sh,' he said, and she sniffed, and stayed where she was, and he let the weight of his arm rest on her back. 'Shh.'

His hand hovered then landed very lightly on top of her spare hand. Morgan was still holding the other one. Ashleigh was in between them, and she didn't move or look up.

'It's OK,' he said. 'It's going to be OK.'

She sighed and stretched out her legs, then raised her head up. They sat watching the good night story for a few more minutes, then Ashleigh spoke again.

'Dad.'

Morgan looked up and she caught the beginnings of a smile on Ashleigh's face.

'I think we can do a lot better than OK,' she said.

ACKNOWLEDGEMENTS

Dedicated to my teenage consultants/personal heroes: Elsa Rowlatt, Zola Rowlatt and Eva Rowlatt.

With endless gratitude to Michael Dean of Andrew Nurnberg Associates, and Will Dady of Renard Press.

Very special thanks to Lucy Potter, Jean Hegland, Jo Young, Barb Turk, Amrita Tripathi, Doug Wallace, Tahmima Anam, Maha Khan, Kamila Shamsie, Ellen Barry, Stephanie Cross, Rachel Holmes, Amy Neil, Barbara Hearn, Helen Reardon Bond, Serena Carr, Lijia Zhang, Laura Fitch, Sarah Gulamhusein, Nick Davis, Nandi Simpson, Amy Frost, Dan Carrier, Domino Pateman, Kate Utley, Talia Barry, Christine Pierce, Claire Roberts Lamont, Nicola Hart, Mr John; Mr Stokes and the staff of Acland Burghley, Catriona Drew, Craig Barker, Chris Goulden and Abigail Scott Paul (formerly of the Joseph Rowntree Foundation), Ezme Selby, Zahrah Rafiq, and last but definitely not least – Justin and Will!

ABOUT THE AUTHOR

Bee Rowlatt is the author of the award-winning travelogue *In Search of Mary*, co-author of the bestselling *Talking About Jane Austen in Baghdad* and contributor to Virago's *Fifty Shades of Feminism*. Bee led the campaign for the Mary Wollstonecraft memorial – the most trolled artwork in living memory – and came out fighting across national and international media. She programmes events at the British Library, and has chaired writers all over the world, been a BBC producer, taught English to the Vice-President of Colombia and worked in a coleslaw factory. Bee is a regular on TV and radio, and has written for the BBC, *Telegraph*, *Times*, *Grazia*, *Die Welt*, *Guardian* and *Daily Mail*. She now lives in London, but hails from Yorkshire, and used to be a showgirl. *One Woman Crime Wave* is her first foray into fiction.

BEEROWLATT.COM 🌐 𝕏 @BEEROWLATT